Ina of Grand Manan

A Stranger from Away

Ina of Grand Manan

A Stranger from Away

Ina Small and Ernie Mutimer

NIMBUS PUBLISHING LIMITED

Nimbus Publishing Limited
P.O. Box 9301, Station A
Halifax, N.S.
B3K 5N5

Cover illustration: Swallowtail Light by Ina Small;
photograph Ernie Mutimer
Cover design: Cardinal Communications, Halifax
Illustrations: paintings by Ina Small; photographs Ernie Mutimer
Photographs: courtesy Ina Small, Gleneta Hettrick, and
Grand Manan Museum
Lyrics at chapter openings: from the operetta *Ina*, copyright © 1988 by
Ernie Mutimer and Robert McMullin

Canadian Cataloguing in Publication Data

Small, Ina

Ina of Grand Manan

ISBN 0-921054-17-3

1. Grand Manan Island (N.B.)—Miscellanea.
I. Mutimer, Ernie. II. Title.

FC2495.G7.S62 1989   971.5'3   C89-098521-9
F1044.G7.S62 1989

Printed and Bound in Canada

Nimbus Publishing Limited gratefully acknowledges the support of the Canada Council and the Nova Scotia Cultural Affairs Division.

For Robert

Acknowledgements

Living more than half a century on Grand Manan, I made many lasting friendships. All the Grand Mananers I knew loved to laugh at themselves, at visitors and, even should they meet, at most people who may read this book.

For sharing their stories freely, I give thanks to Myrtle Anderson Wilcox, Faye Polkinhorn, Gordon Polkinhorn, Archer Wilcox, Leaman Wilcox, Belva Gilmore, Seta Cheney, Johnny Dalzell, Lula Small, Wilfrid Dalzell, Paul Lauzon, Robert Small, and Emma Parker. For their research, I thank Ellen Kierstead, Saint John Public Library, Gleneta Hettrick, Grand Manan Archives, and Wade Reppert.

Ina Small
Saint John, N.B.

Contents

Preface

While the dark clouds of World War I were massing in Europe, five-year-old Ina McAllan left her home in Scotland to travel to Canada. Later, as she attended school in New Brunswick, she dreamed of the enchanting islands in the Bay of Fundy, especially of "her" island, Grand Manan.

All of a sudden Ina was nineteen and a teacher. She travelled to her fantasy island to teach, to fall in love and marry, and to discover in a thousand wonderful ways why the islanders are "a breed apart." After she left Grand Manan, in 1977, she vowed to make the island her final resting place.

My wife, Norah, met Ina McAllan Small some years ago, when she accepted an invitation to tea at Ina's home, then in Queenstown, New Brunswick. They became fast friends almost immediately, for both women were strong, upright, clear eyed, and opinionated. Afterwards Norah insisted we change our holiday schedule in the Maritimes to include a visit to Grand Manan. We were not disappointed. Though progress had brought the questionable modern miracles of electronic communication to the island, its proud people retained their own special identity.

In 1985, now alone, I returned to Ina's home. In the bright kitchen of her two-storey house, on the post road north of the Saint John River, I enjoyed some wonderful home-baked biscuits. As I sipped my third cup of strong tea, Ina mentioned she had compiled a sort of "personal history" of Grand Manan. Was I interested in reading it?

I couldn't put it down. I took the manuscript and embellished it here and there. With the help of a talented Winnipeg musician, Robert McMullin, I also turned it into an operetta whose lyrics open most of the chapters of this book. Here, as in the stage production, fact and fancy mingle: the incidents and anecdotes are part of an enduring impression of a lifestyle tuned to weather and tides.

Grand Manan Island sits at the eastern edge of the border between the United States and Canada, some eight miles off the New Brunswick–Maine coast. About three hundred years ago it appeared on charts as "Menan." Earlier it had been mentioned in Samuel de Champlain's *Voyages,* published in Paris in 1613. Initially he spelled it "Manthane" but in a later edition changed it to "Menane." In any event, the word *Menan* is Passamaquoddy in origin, a corruption of *munanook,* meaning "island place" or "island." The name Grand Manan Island, heard from the lips of strangers and seen in reference works, is actually redundant.

In 1693, as part of New France, Grand Manan was granted to the Sieur de Perigny. But he never officially took possession of the island, so it reverted to France. In 1713, with the signing of the Treaty of Utrecht, the island became British. Nearly a century later the United States claimed it. Following the boundary negotiations of 1817 the United States exchanged it for the British-held Moose Island (on which the American town of Eastport is located) and the smaller Dudley and Frederick islands.

In May 1784, under the leadership of United Empire Loyalist Moses Gerrish, the first permanent settlement was established on Grand Manan. Gerrish was a native of Newberry, Massachusetts, and a graduate of Harvard College. As the only magistrate residing on the island, he was authorized to solemnize marriages. His own wife, ironically, had not joined him in his new home.

Subsequent settlers were predominantly from Maine. Historian Eric Allaby, curator of the Grand Manan Museum, notes that by 1851 the island's population had grown to eleven hundred and its fishing industry had diversified. Over the next thirty years the population more than doubled, remaining relatively constant, at twenty-five hundred, since then. In addition to fishing, the island's mainstays grew to include dulse gathering, forestry, and tourism. As Allaby writes in his book *Grand Manan,* however, the island's resources are "rich, but the special richness is its people." These are the stories of those people, collected over five decades by Ina McAllan Small.

Ernie Mutimer
White Rock, B.C.

Island Dreams

If once you have slept on an island
You'll never be quite the same.
You may look as you looked the day before
And go by the same old name.

You may hustle about in street and shop
You may sit at home and sew
But you'll see blue water and wheeling gulls
Wherever your feet may go.

You may chat with the neighbours of this and that
And close by your fire keep
But you'll hear ship whistles and lighthouse bells
And tides beat through your sleep.

Oh you won't know why and you can't say how
Such change upon you came
But ... once you've slept on an island
You'll never be quite the same.

—Rachel Fields

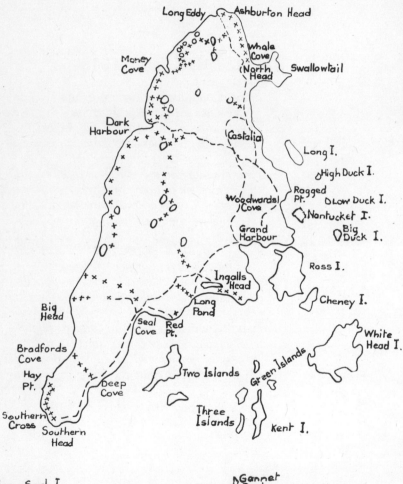

Ina Small's map of Grand Manan

A Stranger from Away

We know you came from Scotland
From far across the foam
So you'll always be a stranger
Though Grand Manan's your home!

I hardly know how to begin, for I don't know when the beginning was. Was it when I was a student at Codys School, on mainland New Brunswick? I remember our geography lessons so well. We learned the counties and their capitals, the towns, the coastal waters, and the islands. We pointed out every one of them on the map, and then we had to draw the whole of New Brunswick from memory. The islands especially fascinated me: Miscou, Portage, Fox, Deer, Campobello, Grand Manan ...

Grand Manan. Somehow that name stood out in my mind. Something about it aroused in me more than simple curiosity. I thought to myself, "Someday I'll visit that island." I never dreamed what an important part it would come to play in my life.

Or was it even earlier? I was born Ina McAllan in Glasgow, Scotland, in December 1906. When I was only five years old, my mother, Elizabeth, brother, William, and I left our homeland. My family had come from upper-class stock, but we had suffered a reverse in fortunes, and my father, William Renton McAllan II, had died. Hurt pride caused my mother to leave her people and her country behind. So in March 1912 we boarded the steamship *Letitia* and set sail for Canada. One of my earliest memories is of that terrible trip. The storms seemed endless, and the weather was bitterly cold. But I never lost my appetite, I was never sick once. For several days I was the only passenger in the dining salon.

"Good morning, Miss McAllan. Enjoy your breakfast." The burr of the bearded captain was as thick as the porridge before me.

"Good morning, Captain," I piped up at the tall, distinguished figure. "And please, steward, may I have three eggs?"

The steward stared at me in disbelief, shaking his head at the captain. "There's a guid girrrl," the captain said. "You're a real sailor! But two eggs wull do!"

In later years, on clear mornings, I watched the steamers sailing across the horizon on their way to Saint John. Was that the way it had been so long ago, when I first crossed the Bay of Fundy? At the end of the voyage, had I actually seen those islands? No matter, the islands of New Brunswick, especially one island, continued to hold me in a spell.

All of a sudden it was 1926. The years had flown by. I was grown up, a full-fledged teacher. My second year of teaching, I applied for a position at Woodwards Cove School, on Grand Manan. Three weeks later a handwritten reply came in the mail from a school trustee, Robert Small:

This is written in response to your recent application for the position of teacher at Woodwards Cove School. I am pleased to inform you that your application is in every way satisfactory, and offer you this position. Please call on me at your earliest opportunity on your arrival to discuss terms and conditions of this appointment.

The writing was neat enough, but I couldn't have cared if it was barely legible. At last I would see that island. I packed and unpacked my meagre wardrobe many times, finally getting my things into some semblance of order. Then I sat on my bed and had second thoughts. I was tired and more than a little apprehensive.

Grand Manan. What would it *really* be like? Perhaps you could climb a big hill at one end and see all the way to the other. Grand indeed. It was that small, I knew.

Small. The name of the school trustee. Would he be old and stern and unable to tolerate a young, relatively inexperienced teacher? "Nonsense, Ina," I said to myself. "Remember, you are a McAllan girl!" I snapped my fingers. "So much for Robert Small!" But life on an island, any island, was bound to be different. I would see water all around. And what about winter? Surely, it would be desolate. I remembered the storms when I sailed aboard the *Letitia.* The island would be bleak enough in such weather. My thoughts frightened me, but I finally went to sleep. I dreamed of the *Letitia* and of two fried eggs staring up at me solemnly from a Donaldson Line platter. "Who says you're a sailor?" said a deep Scottish voice. "We do!" replied twin voices in unison. One of the eggs winked. "After all, she *is* a McAllan."

~

I was just nineteen the day I boarded the *Grand Manan* in Saint John Harbour; it was the Friday before Labour Day, 1926. The ferry had begun service to the island in 1900 as the steamer *Aurora;* her name had been changed in 1911. I found out that fact, together with a good deal of scary fiction, from several other teachers on the same voyage. "Ina ... Ina McAllan," exclaimed one older woman of at least twenty-two years and three full terms' teaching on Grand Manan. "You're not going to Woodwards Cove School are you?" I nodded. "Look out for Robert Small," my new

By 1924 my normal-school friends Edith and Tressa Miller (right) and I (left) were full-fledged teachers.

colleague warned. "He's a regular tyrant." My worst fears were coming true.

"And don't forget the ghost!" exclaimed another.

"G-ghost," I gulped.

"Yes. He visits the school in the middle of winter, right after a blizzard. His face is as white as snow, and he has only two fingers on each hand—frostbite, poor soul. The children are terrified of him."

Fortunately the twinkle in her eye gave this story the lie. I managed to grin weakly. "If he doesn't know the alphabet ... I'll ... I'll shoo him out of my class."

"Good for you, Ina," said the first girl. "By the way, I think you'll like Robert Small. He's really a pet. He lives with his sister, Myra."

Before I could reply, there was a ghostly blast in my ear. I must have jumped a foot. "That's the Long Eddy steam-fog alarm, Ina," said the second teacher, with a knowing yawn meant as much to tease me as anything. "Grand Mananers call it The Whistle." Our ferry gave a loud answering blast as we swung southeast towards the harbour entrance. I jumped again, and my new friends laughed heartily.

Shortly the steamer docked at North Head. It seemed as if everyone on the island had congregated at the jetty. There was a bustle of activity as the ferry was secured and the cargo unloaded.

The second teacher wished me well, went ashore, and was greeted warmly by a handsome young man. I followed the first one across the gangplank, my ears and eyes wide open at the sounds and sights of the wharf. The islanders seemed to have strong American accents. "I'm going to the where," cried out one disembarking passenger. " 'Where?' " I asked. "Don't they know where they're off to?"

"Now, that's the sound of a real Grand Mananer," my friend replied. " 'Where' is the way islanders say *weir*. Every weir has a name. There's Victoria Weir, Bluff Weir, Prescription Weir, and so on." She grinned at me. "Grand Mananers know exactly which weir is where!"

"Hello there!" a loud voice cried out. We both looked around. An elderly man with a weatherworn face and a big smile was leaning out the window of a Model T Ford parked near the end of the jetty.

"Good afternoon, Claude," my friend replied.

"That the new teacher? She's a stranger from away."

"Yes, this is Ina McAllan. She'll be teaching at Woodwards Cove."

"Then I'll be taking her down to Fred's place."

He threw open the door of the Ford and stepped onto the jetty. "Afternoon, miss. Well, how do you like Grand Manan?" I realized he was much younger than I thought. His step was jaunty, and he walked with a rolling gait as he came over and picked up my luggage. He didn't wait for an answer but toted my three bags to the Ford.

"That's the first question they always ask a stranger," my friend said. "Woe betide you if you say, 'Well, it's all right, but....' or 'I can't stand the weather, the fogs are terrible!' They'll ignore you. No one will put themselves out for you." I nodded at this piece of local information. "On the other hand, if you say, 'It's wonderful. I could stay here forever,' or some such words, why, the good news is passed around, and nothing is too much trouble. In plain words, you have it made!" She picked up her single piece of baggage and smiled. "Well, you're on your own, Ina. That's Claude Gilmore. He owns the taxi service, and he's your chance to make a good first impression. One other thing, I'm Olive Coonan. See you!" With that, she strode off towards town.

I walked over to the Ford and climbed in beside Mr. Gilmore. He made no move to get under way. "Well, what do you think?" he asked.

"You know, Mr. Gilmore, when I was just a little girl in school, I used to dream about Grand Manan. And now I'm actually here. I can scarcely wait to explore it."

"That'll do for a stranger from away!" he exclaimed with a wide grin. And we roared off down the island in a cloud of dust.

"Stranger from away." I would hear that expression many times, and it would always tickle me. Eventually I even came to use it myself. Oh, the people were generous, kind, and hospitable, and in times of emergency they were second to none. Yet, in the final analysis, if you were not born on Grand Manan, you were really still a stranger. The island people were intermarried and related to each other—as a Scot, I recognized this as clannishness. For a time you would think you were accepted as one of them. Then should anything come up between you and a native, Grand Mananers would always side with their own. For you were always the stranger from away.

We arrived at my destination. Woodwards Cove was much larger than Codys, where I had grown up, in the heart of New Brunswick farming country. There were about twenty-five houses, mainly of clapboard construction, with different coloured roofs—red, green, grey, black. For each house, there was an outdoor privy. All around the cove, near the school, there were fish stands and wharves; boats were coming and going, rounding the breakwater.

I soon settled in at Fred Small's place, in a bright and cheerful upstairs room. Fred was in his mid-sixties and was indeed related to the school trustee Robert Small—he was his uncle. Next morning I set out to have a good look at the schoolhouse, a large two-storey wooden building with a classroom on each floor. The village's school population having dwindled by about thirty, the upper classroom was bare, no longer in use. This year, there was going to be only one teacher, me, an issue that I planned to raise with Mr. Small.

Meanwhile, I examined every nook and cranny of the down-stairs classroom. With windows on all four sides, I saw that the room would be bright and cheerful. Tight-fitting doors and a large box stove in the centre aisle told me as well that the students would be cosy and warm. Three walls were lined with blackboards, and twenty-five double wooden desks were neatly arranged in rows. Boys' and girls' entrances led to separate cloakrooms, and on a shelf at the back of the room was a galvanized pail with a tin dipper. I made a mental note to appoint a monitor to fetch drinking water from the well of the closest neighbour. In all, the school was in excellent shape, and I was anxious to get to work.

But not before I paid a visit to Mr. Small. In minutes I was knocking on the door of his modest home. A pretty young woman in her early twenties opened it and smiled. I returned the smile. "You must be Miss Myra Small. I'm the new teacher Ina McAllan."

"Come in," she said. Myra called, "Robert, it's a stranger from away!" Then she turned to me and pointed to the kitchen. "Just go through, miss."

When I saw him, he was smoking, poring over a ledger on the kitchen table. He stood, a short five feet six inches. "Good morning, Miss McAllan." He had a fine head of brown hair and deep brown eyes, which I found somewhat disturbing. "Are you settled in at Uncle Fred's?"

"Yes, thank you, I'm quite comfortable." We proceeded to business. I was to receive forty-five dollars a month, and my board was to be two dollars a week. I didn't have to broach the question of the school's not having a second teacher. Mr. Small dealt with that swiftly.

"You have just forty-nine pupils at Woodwards Cove, Miss McAllan," he said matter-of-factly. "Too bad you don't have just one more."

"Why, Mr. Small?"

"Well, then you apply for an assistant."

"You mean if just one family moved into Woodwards Cove, there would be two teachers at the school?"

"That's right." He puffed quietly on a cigarette and waited for my reaction. It seemed unfair, but I changed my mind and decided to say nothing, quite unlike me. In his own way Robert Small was a handsome man. I judged him to be about forty, but he was about to turn thirty-one at the time. He signed my contract, chain-lit another cigarette, and wished me luck. I knew he was busy, so I made my farewells in some confusion. My last thought was that he smoked too much.

I returned to my boarding house in time for lunch. Fred told me that Robert had been working hard since he was fourteen, typical of so many successful men on Grand Manan. He and his brother, Walter, operated a freight boat that carried fish from their weirs to the Maine coast. They also owned a fish factory. I wrinkled my nose at this, as I never could stand the smell of raw fish. The thought of a factory where fish were actually chopped, skinned, and deboned almost made me sick. Needless to say, I didn't eat very much.

～

In the blink of an eye the first day of school rolled around. Boys and girls of all shapes and sizes, in grades 1–8, came and played in the schoolground until it was time for class. Over the Labour Day

My first class at Woodwards Cove School, 1926, consisted of children of all shapes and sizes.

weekend I had spent nearly every hour preparing for this moment, working well after dark and writing notes by the light of my coal-oil lamp. I was feeling a little uneasy, but one thing I did know for sure, I wasn't going to stand for any shenanigans.

I rang the bell loudly, and the children filed quietly into class. They watched me closely as we took stock of each other. "Good morning, children," I said. "My name is Miss McAllan." I turned and wrote it in large letters on the blackboard. "I have all your names here in the register, but I wonder if each of you will stand up and give your name so that I can see who you are." I looked at one boy, who had come to school with his father. "You."

"Wilbur Cossaboom, miss," said the lad, standing up with a broad grin.

Wilbur was quite a character. On my way to school I had met father and son and, making conversation, asked the boy where he was going. Wilbur piped up immediately and, to the shock of his father, replied, "None of your business."

Mr. Cossaboom informed his son in no uncertain terms that this wasn't at all polite. I decided to try out his manners once more, so I asked again. Wilbur gulped and looked at his father, who was watching him sternly. He didn't dare say what he wanted to, so he thought for a moment and then answered, "Who wants to know?"

Opening day went more or less the way I had planned it. My first assignment was on the children's ambitions in life. I wrote carefully on the blackboard, "Put down on your slates what you would like to be doing in ten years' time." The answers told me a good deal about the class. But there was one exception. One lad scrawled, "I want to be a loafer just like my uncle." I watched that boy grow up not to achieve this early ambition. He turned out to be one of the best community workers on the island and an executive with The Bank of Nova Scotia.

Little did I know what was in store for me over the next few weeks. My early English classes were a real indoctrination. *Aspirin* was pronounced "as-pee-in," and *divorce* was pronounced "dis-force." Rich, colourful expressions passed the lips of the children and the adults alike: "Isn't that right, mighty awful" or "We tied the wharf to the boat and went home" or "You stay where you're at, and I'll come to where you're to" or "They sound like tee-hee eggs in a haw-haw's nest" or, my favourite, "Depends on who ya are and who ya ain't."

One morning I had spent a good deal of time on a lesson on nature studies, telling the class how coal was formed over thousands of years. The following day one of my students piped up, "Mees McAllan, about coal, my pa says he don't believe any such damn nonsense." Grand Mananers never *did* stand for nonsense.

Several days later an irate mother was waiting for me when I arrived at school. "Miss McAllan, my boy is practising his arithmetic tables, and he's saying, 'One and one, the son of a bitch is two; two and two, the son of a bitch is four; three and three, the son of a bitch is six ...' And he tells me this is what you told him to say!" I smothered a grin at this startling news. "No, no, I guess he didn't hear me too well. I said, 'The sum of which is two, the sum of which is four,' and so on." She departed much relieved.

Another morning, class was interrupted by a knock on the schoolhouse door. I opened it, and there stood a huge man holding a contrite Joseph Greenlaw by the hand. "Good morning, Miss McAllan," said the giant. "I've brought Joseph back to you. He has a very bad case of schoolitis." He released the boy's hand, and Joseph slunk into class and took his seat. He didn't play truant again, at least not for the rest of the term.

Obviously, I quickly learned that I had to be strict with the children or they would slack off in their studies and misbehave. I soon found out as well that teaching was no nine to four occupation. There were few teachers' aids, and there were lessons to prepare, tests to mark, and examinations to set. I was also expected to tuck in and help at various community functions—it was all part of the job.

Most of all, teachers had to be resourceful. Take Ena Bleumortier, for example. She taught on Inner Wood Island, off the southeast shore. Throughout her tenure she made twenty-five dollars a month; her board was one dollar a week. By the end of the year she managed to save one hundred dollars, which she wisely deposited in the bank.

～

After school I sometimes went to get my mail. The post office was located on the first floor of a two-storey clapboard house; across the aisle was a store, and upstairs was an apartment where the owners lived. The first time I stopped by, the lady behind the wicket was speaking with a customer.

"You must have got up very early this morning, dear."

"No, I didn't," the customer replied. "What makes you say that?"

"Well, you have your dress on inside out."

"I know. The other side is dirty." And she swept out of the store with no little dignity.

The woman behind the wicket then turned to me. "So, you're the new schoolmarm. I hope you're a good one. I'm Alice Draper." I didn't have a chance to reply, as she continued almost without drawing a breath. "Tell me, do you make our kids learn all those dates in the history books?" She obviously expected a reply, for she paused and looked me over. I told her no, that I taught only the important ones. She seemed pleased. "Good. They're a heap o' nonsense. I remember a teacher of mine keeping me in after school because I couldn't remember the date Henry th' Eighth died. And do you know something, no one since has ever asked me when he died!"

Mrs. Draper picked up a bundle of mail and looked through it carefully. "McAllan, McAllan," she muttered. "There's a letter for you, from Eaton's, probably a bill, and here's a postcard from Connie. 'Dear Ina. Glad you are settled in at your boarding house. Glad that you like it at Woodwards Cove. Will be taking the ferry over to see you soon. Love ...' and so on. Connie a good friend of yours?" I nodded as she handed me the mail. "Well, I hope she enjoys her visit. You can call me Alice. You'll be missing your old friends, seeing as how you're a stranger from away."

～

In the early fall, when I wasn't working, I explored the island from top to bottom. In all, there were six villages on the east coast. On the northeastern edge was North Head, where the ferry docked, at Steamboat Wharf; then moving south down the main road was Castalia, Woodwards Cove, Grand Harbour, Ingalls Head, and

Seal Cove. These towns varied in population from as few as fifty to as many as six hundred; even these numbers jumped up and down as islanders moved from one place to another. (At one time, before I arrived, Woodwards Cove was the biggest and busiest settlement on the island.) There was also Deep Cove, south of Seal Cove and more a hamlet than a village; Dark Harbour, a small settlement on the west coast; and Southern Head, a cluster of homes for the keepers of Southern Head Light.

On weekends I made my way around the rugged shoreline at Woodwards Cove to Ragged Point, where the rocks rise up like mountains. I climbed them many times, and on clear days I could see Long, Low Duck, High Duck, Big Duck, and Nantucket islands, a handful of the archipelago of some twenty islands off Grand Manan's east coast.

I discovered the Seven Days Work, a layered rock formation near Whale Cove, above North Head. On the back part of Grand Manan I was awed by the cliffs, ranging in height from 250 to 400 feet. The Boy Scouts had marked many trails, which I followed all by myself. Heading towards Seal Cove, I turned east off the Red Head Road and went to Red Point. I found an unusual rock formation where grey lava had flowed over red sedimentary rock. I ran into amateur geologists, we chatted for a few moments, and then I was on my way.

Between Grand Harbour and Castalia I came across a high hill that Fred called Bald Mountain. When I saw it, I knew I had to climb it. It wasn't easy, but I approached it carefully, and after a stiff climb I was rewarded with a spectacular view from North Head all the way to the southern part of the island. Another time, I walked from North Head to The Whistle, which looks towards Eastport and Lubec, Maine. It was clear that day, and, peering right, I could make out the faint shoreline of Nova Scotia. All the while, The Whistle gave out its eerie sound to warn passing ships of the huge cliff looming ahead, the sound that had so frightened me on my voyage to Grand Manan. It could be heard for miles.

On sunny days my autumn explorations were always happy. Often, though, the fog rolled in; sometimes it was light, sometimes it was as thick as pea soup. The fog was bad enough, but as the herring boats made their way past the breakwater to the harbour, the screech of thousands of hungry gulls made me feel weird and empty. It was a melancholy sound like a dirge, uttered for all the people who had been lost at sea—or so I imagined.

~

The next time I went for my mail, Alice Draper had another card from Connie. "Says she'll be over on next Monday's ferry," Alice reported. "Hope the weather will be nice for her." There were several other people in the post office at the time, including one stranger. Then in walked a fisherman who *Reader's Digest* later named one of the most unforgettable characters in the world. Gleason Green of Ingalls Head had a delightful habit of boasting. As Fred had told me, this man's boat was faster than anyone else's, his car was bigger, and his catch was larger. But today he was going to meet his match. After wishing us all good afternoon, Gleason walked right up to the stranger, looked at him carefully, and slowly shook his head.

"Well?" Alice asked.

"I don' know 'im. Guess he's a stranger from away."

The stranger smiled as we all chuckled.

"How are you?" Gleason asked, holding out his hand.

"Well, let me tell you I'm one of the luckiest men you could meet," the stranger replied, taking the outstretched hand and shaking it heartily.

"How's fishing?"

"Wonderful. I've never had better catches in my life. Nets brim full every haul. As for the lobsters, I just can't keep emptying my traps fast enough!"

"You must be doing well?"

"I'm next to being a millionaire!"

"I'm glad to hear that."

"Why?"

"Well, I'm from the income-tax department," Gleason said. Silence fell in the post office. The stranger's face fell, too. "Wanna know something else?" Gleason asked.

The man nodded. "Sure."

"I'm the biggest damn liar on Grand Manan!"

Blessed Be the Ties that Bind

God will save me from the flood
And Satan's hosts will drown
Showers, showers of blessing
From heaven will pour down

Connie looked lovely. She wore a smart white dress with a pink sash that matched her shoes and gloves; a broad-brimmed hat was set on her head at a jaunty angle. She gingerly removed the hat pin and carefully took off the hat as we sat down to tea. She was staying with her aunt and uncle Anita and Perry Mason (P.M.) Small in Woodwards Cove.

Connie Lambert and I were old friends. We had attended normal school together, and she, too, had chosen teaching as her vocation. She had a real love for Grand Manan and had visited it many times. She had more relatives on the island—her other aunt and uncle, Edna and Chester Tatton, lived in the north; Chester was the keeper of The Whistle.

Connie asked me how school was going, gave me all the gossip from the mainland, and then began to talk about the island. "People here are quite different, Ina."

"I know that already, Connie."

"They're self-reliant and independent. You'll find you can get wonderful service from the odd-job man, the carpenter, or plumber, but only when they find it convenient to do the work. It doesn't matter if you're a millionaire or a pauper, everything will be done in turn. You'll need to develop a lot of patience." I smiled at that, for Connie knew I was rather short tempered and impatient at times.

She sipped her tea and continued. "Not too long ago an island man said to me, 'I go when I want to, where I want to. Nobody tells me what to do.' If you expect things done right away, no matter what, you're in for a shock, Ina."

"I like the people just the way they are," I protested. "Honestly."

"That'll do for a stranger from away." She laughed.

I laughed, too. That's what Claude Gilmore had said to me the day I arrived. I remembered his rolling gait as he walked over to me. That's how the men of the island often walked, with a rolling gait, as though they were on the deck of a boat. They strolled along with their hands in their pockets. They were in no hurry; they took their own good time.

"I just hope too many tourists don't settle here," Connie rattled on.

"Yes, that would spoil everything. It's almost as if ... as if every man here is a king."

Connie looked at me solemnly. "Tell me, Ina McAllan, have you found your own prince charming?"

"What a thing for you to ask!"

"Answer the question, Ina."

"Honestly, Connie, I can't ... at least ... not yet." The conversation drifted away to less dangerous shoals, even though an image of a certain school trustee flickered through my mind. I blushed inwardly.

~

That must have been some sort of premonition, for soon after Connie's visit I received a gentleman caller at school. It was Robert Small. He stood at the door, cap in hand, shifting his weight from one foot to the other.

"Good day, Mr. Small. What can I do for you?" He hummed and hawed a bit, and the children started to giggle. "Be quiet, class," I scolded. "Get along with your exercise." I moved outside, and the poor man's tongue untied enough for him to stammer out an invitation. "I was wondering, Miss McAllan, if you'd care to go to the dance with me next Saturday. It's at the Knights of Pythias."

Well, I hummed and hawed a bit myself. I hadn't expected him to be so direct. Finally I told him I'd be delighted. I shot back to class, leaving him standing with one foot on the front steps. The children stopped murmuring, but most of them stared at me with broad grins. They'd easily guessed Mr. Small's intentions. To hide my embarrassment, I immediately gave them a tough spelling test. By the time the midday break arrived, I was quite composed.

Social life on Grand Manan was active, to say the least. Parties were held in homes and halls, lively affairs with boisterous games and rousing singsongs. The Masons, Rebeccas, and Knights of Pythias were all going concerns, augmented shortly by the Order of the Eastern Star and the Knights of Pythias Sisters. Every order held wonderful socials, each trying to outdo one another's clam or fish chowders or lobster stews, served in great abundance to eager guests.

These occasions did not include glasses of whiskey or rum. Officially the island was dry, and most people, publicly at least, were opposed to liquor. But don't think they didn't have their liquor. Oh no! They smuggled it onto Grand Manan from Eastport and Lubec. There were several well-known island bootleggers, too, and after Prohibition liquor was always available from the Steamboat Wharf agent at North Head.

I could hardly wait until the Knights of Pythias dance. There was more than a touch of frost in the air when Robert arrived early that evening. He was driving an ancient open-sided Ford sedan, and beside him, on the seat, was a musical-instrument case that turned out to contain a tenor saxophone.

Much to my dismay, my date was a member of the Knights of Pythias band. He spent most of the night with the rest of the group, blowing away on his saxophone. But the music was loud and lively, and fortunately I had no shortage of dance partners. Fox trots and waltzes and two-steps followed one after another, and every now and then the band played a social one-step, giving me the opportunity to meet more young men. What with the quadrilles and lancers, I soon danced with everyone in the hall. When it was all over, I was more than a little smug, for I rather thought I'd been the belle of the ball. As for Robert, he had very little to say on the drive home. Somehow I felt he wasn't any too pleased that I hadn't spent the evening mooning over the sweet sounds of the Knights of Pythias orchestra. When he dropped me off at home, though, I knew I would be seeing him again.

~

Through Connie I had become friendly with P.M. and Anita Small. Anita was a teacher, and P.M. was a fisherman and a customs officer. One Sunday I was invited to join them for dinner and to accompany them to church. Religion was a cornerstone of life on Grand Manan. Settlers had built the first place of worship in 1823: St. Paul's Anglican Church in Grand Harbour. (The old wooden church had burned down, and in 1840 a stone building had replaced it.) By the 1920s, in Woodwards Cove, there were actually six denominations—Advent, Pentecostal, Roman Catholic, Jehovah's Witness, Wesleyan Baptist, and Anglican—and for nearly every denomination, there was a church. (The Anglicans congregated in the Advent church, an early example of the ecumenical movement.) As one choir sang "Will There Be Any Stars in My Crown?," another sang "No! No! Not One!"

After dinner we quickly cleared the dishes and started walking to St. Paul's. About halfway there, Anita quietly asked P.M. if he had brought the collection.

"Yes," he replied.

"How much?"

"Well, I got one cent, ten cents, a quahtah, and a dollah."

"What are you going to put in?"

"Depends."

"On what?"

St. Paul's Anglican Church, Grand Harbour, is the oldest place of worship on Grand Manan.

"Well, if that ministah gives in a good sermon, I'll put in the dollah. If he don't, then I'll jist drop in what I think it's worth."

We soon came to the church. We took our places, and the service began. The preacher started on a long, drawn-out sermon. "Peter's wife's mother lay sick of the fever," he droned. At long last the sermon ended, and the ushers started to take up the collection. P.M. elbowed me and whispered, "Say, Ina, have you got change for a cent?"

Later that afternoon, there was a revival at the Pentecostal Assembly, in Woodwards Cove. Though it depended on the mood of the congregation, the revivals were usually loose in structure, consisting of public testimonies, or confessions, a sermon, and lots of boisterous singing. Most Grand Mananers were not bound to visit just one church, and everyone loved the evangelists, never missing the revivals. The more secular islanders went for the sheer joy of the events, to clap their hands and stamp their feet to the high tempo of the music. To this extent their participation was sincere, even though their theology was on somewhat shaky ground.

I decided to go and see for myself. The testimonies seemed to be prompted more by a sense of fun than by true belief. One man said he was so full of the Holy Spirit that without knowing it, he had walked over a huge woodpile in his bare feet. At this a young woman cried out, "I feel so unworthy that I believe I should hide behind that door!" Another young man jumped to his feet, almost stumbling in his eagerness. "Dear brothers and sisters," he testified, "I, too, feel unworthy, so unworthy that I should be put behind that door with our beloved sister!"

This ended the testimonies for the moment. The preacher took a tiny pitch pipe out of his pocket and sounded a note. We all sang "Shall We Gather at the River." The song concluded with a hearty chorus, and then the preacher cleared his throat. "And now my message for today: 'Peter's wife's mother lay sick of the fever.'" My eyes widened.

His message was short and snappy, an abridged version of the one given at St. Paul's. Yet I could tell that the preacher was greatly moved, and many in the congregation were actually in tears. The evangelist seized the opportunity to call for an affirmation of faith. "All of you who believe in the Lord and love the Lord," he urged, "stand on your feet and be counted!"

Every one of us stood, except one old man. The preacher walked quickly down the aisle and went up to him. "Well," he asked in thunderous tones, "aren't *you* a Christian?"

"I think I am," said the old man.

"Then, why are you not standing?"

"I don't care to."

"Wouldn't you stand up if the dear Lord wanted you to do so?"

"Of course."

The preacher repeated the question slowly. "Then, *why* are you not standing?"

"Well, I thought it was only you wanted me to stand."

"Oh no. Brothers and Sisters, let's all sing 'Stand Up, Stand Up for Jesus!' Let's hear it for the Lord!" Again he sounded his pitch pipe. We all sang uproariously, even the old man.

The preacher was young and enthusiastic. But he was also human. We all knew he was courting a pretty young girl in the congregation. She always wore a hood.

When the hymn finished, the preacher noticed that the old man was now at the back of the church, smoking a pipe. The preacher was horrified. "Why, Brother, you're smoking! During testimony you said you were living as close to the dear Lord as you could get. Smoking is a sin!"

"Jolstay,* I am!" said the sinner, knocking out his pipe on a pew.

"You should be ashamed of yourself, Brother!"

"Jolstay, I am, Reverend. And if I had a hood, I would have it down over my face!"

*Jolstay *is a fisherman's expression meaning "golly," "I'll say," or "damn it all, anyway."*

This set the congregation abuzz. There were some veiled whispers and a number of loud nervous coughs. I looked around, and several of the less devout members were chuckling.

"Haven't you found Jesus Christ?" persisted the young evangelist desperately.

"Didn't know he was lost, didn't know he was lost."

"You're lost, Brother, unless you mend your ways. Pray for our poor brother, friends, pray for him." The preacher held up both arms, beseeching us.

"Amen, amen," the congregation sang. "Save him, Lord!"

Somewhat more in control, the evangelist returned to the front of the church. "I want to thank you, Lord, for your love and goodness!"

"Hallelujah. Praise the Lord. Amen," the congregation recited.

"Next Sunday, God willing, we shall have not one but two services of baptism."

"Hallelujah. Praise the Lord. Amen."

"We shall hold these services at North Head and at Seal Cove so children can be baptized at both ends."

Funerals were as popular as revivals—everyone knew when they were, where they were, and who was being buried. All the neighbours pitched in, digging the grave, and cooking the food for callers, a custom that still prevails. Johnny Graham of Castalia was the undertaker; in 1905, at sixteen, he had taken over his father's business. For a modest fee that usually depended on the circumstances of the customer, he supplied the coffin, services, and direction. (Sometimes he didn't charge at all, and in 1971 Grand Mananers honoured his generosity by throwing a birthday party for him.) The deceased was then taken by horse-drawn hearse to the cemetery, with mourners walking slowly behind. This reminded me of the Highlands of Scotland, where processions were led by a piper playing a lament.

The day after the revival I was walking down the road in Woodwards Cove when a funeral procession ambled past. I was daydreaming about Scotland as I came across the old man who had been smoking in church. He was seated on an old crate. "Good afternoon," I said. "Who passed away?"

"Well," said the old man, "I was at three services yesterday, and each preacher read the very same text. So I guess it must be Peter's mother-in-law, seeing how she was dying all day." We both laughed. He lit his pipe and chuckled again. We watched as the cortege disappeared around a bend in the road. "Saw you at two

of 'em, teacher. Not bad for a stranger from away." He drew deeply
on his pipe. "Want to hear my favourite mother-in-law story?"

"All right," I said and sat down on an overturned cask next to
him.

"Well," said my new friend, "it seems this here fisherman down
at Seal Cove sure hated his mother-in-law. He wasn't happy when
his wife told him the old lady was going to pay them a visit. Anyway,
the old woman got the ferry at Saint John. Now, the cabin was hot,
and she felt a little sick, so she went up on deck for some fresh air.
She was leaning over the rail when the ferry hit a big wave and
bounced. Over went the old woman into the Bay of Fundy.

"You can bet the man was glad when the ferry was late. Later he
got a telegram: 'Regret inform you mother-in-law drowned. Body
recovered, ten lobsters attached. Please advise.'" He put some
more tobacco in his pipe and tamped it down. "Now, it didn't take
but a moment for that fisherman to send a reply: 'Please ship
lobsters here, and set the old woman agin!'"

The old man chuckled to himself, stood, and walked slowly back
to a small house that was under construction. A few hand tools
were scattered about, and he picked up a saw and started to cut
a piece of planking. I was amazed. He looked well into his
seventies, yet he was building himself a house. "Call me Uncle
Willie," he shouted.

My curiosity was overwhelming, so I walked over to him. "How
come you're building a house at your time of life?" He laid down the
saw and paced slowly back and forth, flapping his coat tails with
his hands, almost as a bird flaps its wings. Then he stopped and
looked me in the eye. "Well, teacher, I'm too old a man to be livin'
out of doors, so I am, so I am." I found out eventually that he was
seventy-five, a mighty age for someone to be building his own
house.

Uncle Willie was what most people would call a religious
dilettante. He attended nearly every service, even those of the
Salvation Army when it first came to Grand Manan, in the 1880s.
According to Uncle Willie, a lot of locals had no use for the
Salvationists. In the beginning the Army held its meetings over
Peter Dixon's store. Then it moved to the Happy Hour Theatre,
built in North Head before the turn of the century. Finally, about
1900, it built its own hall. There the Army usually had a full house,
for many curious islanders wanted to find out what it stood for.

This curiosity did not please a certain group of four men and a
teenage boy. They decided to take matters into their own hands
and drive the Salvation Army off Grand Manan for good. The upper
floor of the Salvation Army citadel was unfinished. One day, when

the hall was empty, the five schemers wrestled a handful of large hogsheads up to the second floor and mounted them on a large plank supported by two trestles. The plank was attached to a pole that, in turn, was fastened to a long rope. They fed the rope through a hole bored in the eaves so that it hung down the side of the building. The evening before the rally they stole a horse and wagon and spent most of the night hauling water to fill the hogsheads.

The crowd at the Salvation Army meeting was especially large— Uncle Willie barely managed to find a seat. Outside, the five sinners resolutely resisted all summons to the seat of mercy as they waited for the service to end. As the meeting closed, with a rousing rendition of "Showers of Blessings," they pulled on the rope. The pole tipped the plank—and the hogsheads.

"By God, Ina," Uncle Willie recalled, "there was a sound like mighty thunder, and all of a sudden it began to rain right inside the building! Some folks thought it was a miracle!" As the water continued to pour through the cracks in the ceiling, showering a dubious blessing on the congregation below, the meeting broke up in some confusion. There was utter consternation as people ran out of the hall.

That wasn't the end of the story, not as far as Uncle Willie was concerned. The five pranksters got away scot-free that night, but then things, strange things, started to happen. Some time later three of the men drowned. The fourth man became a cripple and died after a lingering illness. As for the boy, he became so scared of water that he never went out in a boat or even crossed a frozen pond. The Salvation Army, however, undampened by the unseasonable indoor shower, grew in strength and numbers.

～

Besides Uncle Willie and P.M. and Anita Small, I had come to know many other villagers. Billy Kiscadden, a middle-aged fisherman, was one man who gave me no peace. He teased me mercilessly about everything: my playing the organ at school concerts, my singing—he told everyone that I sang to myself—and my male friends. He just wouldn't let up.

I decided to take my revenge. Like most islanders, Fred Small had a vegetable garden and a cow, and he supplied some locals with milk. They dropped off quart lard kettles, and he filled them. One Saturday night I saw a kettle of milk out on the platform in front of the house. I knew at once that it belonged to Billy. He and his wife were up at North Head, playing bridge with friends. They would come by for the milk quite late, on their way home.

It was the moment of truth. I went into the house, got some bits of twine, tied them together to make one long piece, and fastened one end to the kettle. I tucked the length of twine under the boards of the porch and attached the other end to the doorknob. I barely had time to hide when I heard Billy's car rattling down the road.

He stopped outside Fred's house, climbed out of his car, and strode up the walk to the porch, whistling a merry tune. I waited breathlessly. He reached down, picked up the kettle, and walked jauntily back down the walk. When he was halfway to his car, he stopped short—the twine had jerked the kettle out of his hand, and milk had spilled in all directions. I heard him cussing to his wife when he found the twine. Not a single lamp was lit in Fred's place, so Billy got in his car and drove off in high dudgeon.

Next morning it was early when Billy stormed into the kitchen waving the empty milk kettle. I awoke to hear him complaining to Fred in a loud voice, "That schoolma'am so-and-so ..." Then he came to the foot of the stairs and yelled up at me, "I'll get even with ya!" I was all innocence of course. But word spread quickly that the new teacher had given Billy Kiscadden his "come-uppance."

Feeling smug, I got up and got ready to go to Sunday service. Before breakfast I went outdoors to take a deep breath of the fresh fall air. All of a sudden, there was a strange clanking on the road. I looked up, and Uncle Willie was passing by, dragging a long chain.

"Good morning," I cried. "Do you belong to a chain gang?"

He grinned at me and came over to the gate. "Mornin', Ina," he called. "On my way to early service." He rattled the long chain. "Blessed be the ties that bind!" We both laughed.

"How's old Sal?" I asked.

Uncle Willie loved animals. He had a horse named Sally—Sal he called her. She was past her working days, but Uncle Willie kept her around as a pet, as he couldn't bear to part with her. Now and again he hitched her up to his buggy and took her out for a little exercise.

"She ain't ready for the glue factory yet," he said. "Took her for a run to Seal Cove the other day."

Then he launched into one of his stories. "I know a young fella at Seal Cove always dragged a chain with him. Rattled it, sang to it, tooted at it, made believe it was his car. Even took it to service with him. Used to park it outside the church door. After morning prayer he'd pick it up again, make more car noises, and then away he'd go. Well, the minister got real curious about all this, so one Sunday he asked, 'Tell me, young fella, why do you always drag that chain behind you?' Quick as a wink the young buck replied, 'It's this way, Minister. Did you ever try pushin' a chain in front of you?' "

Uncle Willie looked at me solemnly for all of ten seconds before his face lit up with a huge grin. "See you in church, Ina." And off he went merrily down the road, puffing on his pipe and dragging the chain behind him.

Settling Down

It was time to fall in love
And dream of stars and moon above ...
Now the news is all around
Robert Small will settle down

In spite of regular attendance at nearly every church on the island, Uncle Willie managed to find time to close in his new place before the cold weather set in. There he lived, snug and happy, smoking his pipe and occasionally enjoying the odd chaw of "terbacca." Like most islanders, he never locked the front door. There was really no need to, which was just as well because not a single policeman could be found from Seal Cove to North Head. In fact, the first RCMP officer didn't come to Grand Manan until 1932. His name was R.K. Ackman, and he drove an old Ford coach.

Soon after Uncle Willie had moved in, however, there was an incident. Two fellows were passing by, and seeing a light in the cabin window, they decided to play a prank. They reversed the car and drove right up to the front door, so close that the door couldn't be opened. Then they blasted the horn. They thought that this was hilarious until the door opened—inwards. There stood Uncle Willie with a shotgun in his hands. The screech of rubber as those two young men took off would have wakened the dead. Uncle Willie, as usual, was unperturbed. "Course the gun wasn't loaded, Ina," he chuckled. "But they sure as hell didn't know that!"

That fall I tried to see as much of Uncle Willie as I could. But I had a busy social calendar, for I had a number of men friends. As I had predicted, however, Robert Small was the most persistent. Having learned his lesson, he was careful to take me to dances *not* held by the Knights of Pythias. Neither of us missed his saxophone.

He also took me to the movies. We went to the Happy Hour Theatre—a second theatre was built in the forties, in Grand Harbour—where we saw silent films with Douglas Fairbanks and Mary Pickford, Charlie Chaplin, Buster Keaton, or William Hart.

By early 1927 I guess you could say we were going steady. One January evening we went skating. The air was crystal cold and clear, and as Robert took my arm and we skated along, it seemed as though we were flying. Faster and faster we skated, the steam of our breath trailing far behind and floating into the darkness. I'll never forget that night.

I started going steady with Robert within six months of my arrival.

While we were courting, I heard plenty of stories about other couples in town. When Chester Guptill was dating his wife-to-be, Eula Russell, cars were few and far between. So Chester decided to take her to a dance in style. He asked Uncle Willie if he could borrow his horse, Sal.

"Uncle Willie, I want to ask you a favour."

"Go ahead," the old man replied.

"I want to go to the dance at North Head tonight, and I wondered if I could hire Sal?"

"My gosh, man," chuckled Uncle Willie, "what do you want to hire my nag fer? She can't dance a step."

As Uncle Willie was telling me the story, I noticed he was resting his leg on a stool. Sal was usually pleasant, but in one of her rare bad-tempered moments, she had kicked the old man. I asked him what had happened. "Mosquito bite, Ina," he said, rolling up his trouser leg to show a nasty bruise and large laceration. "Yep, it was some mosquito. It had to fold its wings just to get through the door."

～

Some romances were not so legitimate as ours and Chester and Eula's. Take one woman who was rather liberal with her sexual favours. Her fee, I'm told, was twenty-five cents. She was, I suppose, the original "two-bit hooker."

This woman, who shall remain nameless, had several children by different fathers. Visiting a neighbour one day, she confessed she was worried about her daughter.

"Why?" asked the neighbour.

"Well, it's this way," the hooker replied. "She hasn't had any children yet."

"Is that right? How long has she been married?"

"Oh no, she ain't married."

Another woman was a housekeeper for a Seal Cove man for many years. Friends and neighbours alike teased them about not getting married, but both parties stoutly denied any sexual intimacy. A ghostly apparition eventually gave this the lie.

One morning the housekeeper rushed over to her neighbour. "What a dreadful night it was!" she exclaimed.

"What do you mean? It was calm and quiet, and there was a beautiful moon."

"Yes, it was, but I heard it plainly, I know I did. Footsteps … ghostly footsteps along the beach."

"What did you do?" asked the neighbour.

"Well, I leaned over in bed and nudged the old man awake, and he got up and went out, but he couldn't see nothin' at all."

~

Time flew by, and one morning I looked out my window and saw the familiar V of Canada geese. Spring had come to Grand Manan. Soon every small boat on the island would be due for attention. First, each fisherman scraped the sides and bottom of his boat to remove seaweed and slime. Then, he drove caulking compound or oakum into the seams. Finally, he gave the boat two coats of marine finish, usually white. Only the trim varied on each craft, providing a rainbow of colours on the sea. Even the ferry got time off in the spring for a paint job, leaving smaller boats such as the *Pride of Fundy* to bring freight to the island.

Homes on Grand Manan also received their regular quota of paint, especially those near the water. The sea blast was as hard on houses as the sea itself was on boats. Most islanders painted their houses white, but the odd Grand Mananer showed horrible taste.

Marian Bristol, a retired dietician from New York, was driving down the island with two friends, Perley and Jennie Lambert (no relation to my friend Connie Lambert) of North Head. Aunt Jennie, as she was known, was the secretary of an informal women's group nicknamed The Glass-Eye Society—all its members wore glasses—which did community work such as making sure the Anglican

Church of the Ascension Cemetery, in North Head, was maintained. This organization had also built the Happy Hour Theatre.

The Lamberts were devout and kept the Sabbath faithfully. As they passed through one village, the couple was shocked to see a nephew out painting his house. Those things were just not done on Sunday. "My, my," cried Aunt Jennie, "that is awful!" Painting on the Sabbath is what Jennie meant, but not Marian, who was staring in horror at the yellow house, the red roof, the green trim, and the blue foundation. "Yes, indeed," sighed the dietician, "those sure *are* God-awful colours!"

~

As summer rolled around, I began to pack for the mainland. My brother, William, had invited me to spend July and August with him at his home in Queenstown, on the mainland. Robert asked if he could write me while I was away, and of course I said yes. Our correspondence kept our romance alive over the holidays, and when I returned in the fall, Robert greeted me warmly.

One Saturday night we went to see a William Hart movie. Both Robert and I loved westerns, but don't ask me now what the movie was all about. What I do remember is holding hands and whispering things that at the time meant the world to both of us. On the way home Robert proposed. Well, eventually.

"Ina, do you think I should fix up the old house in town?"

"No, Robert, I don't."

"No?"

"No."

"Well," he stammered, "what do you think of a new house?"

"Sounds wonderful."

He finally summoned enough courage to plunge ahead. "Now, listen to me, Ina McAllan, if I build you a brand new house in Woodwards Cove, would you stay on Grand Manan ... and ... and ... marry me?"

My heart leapt at his words, but my innate Scottish prudence tempered my reply. "I'll consider that, Robert."

Well, there it was, as strong an affirmation as I was prepared to give until specific details of our engagement could be worked out. But it was good enough for Robert. He stopped the car and kissed me on the spot. Any reticence I had against a marital alliance melted in an instant. I said yes.

I was committed to marry a fisherman. What would my poor mother say? I could almost hear her words: "Ina, Ina, there's no a mon in the colonies that's guid enough for my bra'e girrrl. Never, never a lazy, lousy fisherman. Wha's gotten inta my girrrl?" Mother had been raised in a castle, and her bonnie Scottish heart knew only one kind of fisherman, the shiftless louts who were the vagabonds of Highland ports and taverns. She could have no inkling of Robert's very real success—he owned weirs, a factory, and a house—and, to be honest, his success as an island businessman played no little part in my decision. It certainly made up for the eleven-year difference in our ages, for my Scottish practicality told me he was a far better catch than some unproven twenty-year-old lad.

I had a sudden qualm. "I can never work in the factory, Robert." Most of the island women worked in the fish factories.

"I'll never ask you to, Ina." And he never did.

In October, Robert gave me a simple engagement ring, and I wore it publicly for the first time to the Hallow'een dance at the Masonic Hall in Woodwards Cove. But before we even announced the engagement, tongues started to wag.

"Hey, Ina," said Uncle Willie one afternoon, "I hear someone's going to be buildin' a new house in town. Now, I wonder who's going to be livin' there?" He fixed his gaze on me.

"I'm sure I don't know, Uncle Willie," I said uncomfortably.

"Thought you did, Ina, thought you did." Off he went up the road, whistling "Roses Are Blooming in Picardy."

Billy Kiscadden went on the offensive soon after he heard the news. "Don't mean to spill the milk, Ina, if you know what I mean, but when's the house goin' to be built?" Billy was finally having his revenge.

~

When we were first engaged, Robert took it on himself to teach me how to drive. He took me out in his old Ford sedan, with its open sides, and sat me behind the wheel. (I've often thought since that we should have kept that venerable antique: it would be worth a pretty penny these days.) Robert was patient, and I was determined. So in spite of my sometimes short temper at all things mechanical, I soon mastered the intricacies of clutch and gearbox and was clattering up and down the dirt roads of Grand Manan like an old hand.

One other female pioneer had never had a car out by herself, but she decided to be brave one day and drive from Ingalls Head to Grand Harbour, about two miles. On her way home she was doing well until she saw another car approaching. She was nearing the intersection of the Grand Harbour Road and the Thoroughfare Road. Though she had it in her mind to turn, the approaching auto caused her to have second thoughts. So she pulled into Will Cronk's driveway.

Robert, I, and friends enjoyed many outings in the open-sided Ford.

Will was a Grand Harbour fisherman, and he never did think too much of women drivers. He watched as she backed out several times, still finding herself going the wrong way. She couldn't get the car turned around. Finally Will couldn't stand it any longer. He stuck his head out the door of his house and yelled, "My God, woman! Where in the hell do you want to go?"

"Oh, Mr. Cronk," she cried, "I want to go down island, but this cussed car seems to have a mind of its own!"

Uncle Willie had one or two experiences with those early days of motoring. Once, he hitched a ride with a visiting "drummer," or travelling salesman, who had brought his Buick over on the ferry. As they approached North Head, the salesman was complaining about all the jaywalkers. Just at that moment an old man stepped out onto the road. The salesman blasted his horn, but the aged pedestrian looked him in the eye and walked right in front of the car. Hopping mad, the salesman hit the brakes and screeched to a stop. He leapt out of his car and gave the old man a real lecture. The old man smiled at him and walked away, into the McLean store. Uncle Willie started to laugh. "What's so funny?" the salesman asked, getting back into the car and slamming the door. "Don't you know?" chuckled Uncle Willie. "That old fella, he's stone deaf!"

In the 1940s the roads were hard-surfaced, a great boon to motoring—before, in the spring, the roads turned to bogs. But the young people used to walk on the first pavements as if there were no cars at all. I often had to swerve to avoid hitting them. Then one day I was driving just outside Grand Harbour when I came across four lads strung side by side across the road. They were coming towards me, and they showed no sign of moving, so I stopped the car. They had to walk around me, in single file, where they should have been in the first place. As one boy passed by, he complained, "What d' ya mean hoggin' all the road?" Now, I ask you!

Paved roads also made it easier to speed. Gleason Green, the boasting fisherman, was a little cavalier behind the wheel. He was taking his sick brother to the hospital in Saint John. Having cleared the ferry, he put on quite a burst of speed. Just by McKay's Diner in Pennfield, near Blacks Harbour, he was hauled over by an RCMP cruiser.

"What's your hurry, sir?" the young Mountie asked politely. "You were doing seventy through a forty zone." Gleason explained that his brother was sick. "Sorry to hear that, sir," the officer said. "Can I escort you into the city?" The Grand Mananer looked at the Mountie's Ford, patted his Plymouth on the flank, and replied, "We both thank you, Constable, but you'd be right in my way."

～

In the spring of 1928 Robert contracted with a fine craftsman, Cecil Graham of Castalia, to build our home. By then I had been teaching at Woodwards Cove School for nearly two years, with a raise that had brought my salary up to fifty-five dollars. One afternoon an old friend of mine called. It was George Mitchell, whom I'd known on the mainland.

"Ina," he said, "I've been at Castalia School for three years. I'm leaving at the end of the term. They'll be looking for another teacher. There are fewer pupils than at Woodwards Cove *and* the pay is better! Why don't you apply?"

I thanked George and put in my application. In my interview the trustees at Castalia told me they'd be happy to hire me, for, they said, I had the reputation of being both an excellent teacher and a firm disciplinarian. It was music to my ears. What's more, the salary was sixty-five dollars a month, a raise of more than 18 percent! That warmed the cockles of my Scottish heart.

The school secretary, Arthur Richardson, shook hands with me and showed me around the school. Like Woodwards Cove School, it had only two rooms, but they were both on the ground floor. Again, I would be the only teacher; again, I would have grades 1–8.

Robert and I were supposed to be married in August, but the house wasn't finished, so for the fall term in Castalia, I obtained room and board at Johnny Dalzell's, still paying only two dollars a week.

When Johnny wasn't fishing, he was selling sewing machines and pianos. He was a crack salesman because he was a good storyteller who made friends easily. Often he brought his new acquaintances home to dinner. This was a constant source of embarrassment to his wife, Lydia, who did not always prepare enough to feed extra mouths.

Typical was the time he brought home a visitor from the mainland. The guest enjoyed the whole meal immensely, especially the dessert, an apple-crisp pie. "Have another piece," said Johnny. Lydia kicked him under the table.

"Well, I must admit that that pie is the finest I've ever tasted," said the guest, wiping a crumb from his mouth.

"I insist you have seconds." Johnny was all smiles until he received an urgent kick from Lydia that made him wince. "Stop kicking me under the table, woman!" he bellowed.

"I see I now have your attention, Johnny," Lydia said politely. "I'm sorry, but there is no more pie."

Meals were never dull at the Dalzell home. When Johnny's nephew Russell Graham stayed for dinner, there was the usual ample spread. As Lydia served Russell, she asked him if he liked potatoes and turnips. Young Russell nodded, so he received a generous helping of each. When the meal was over, the boy had not touched his turnips. "Why, Russell," Lydia cried, "I thought you said you liked turnips?"

"I do, Auntie, I do," he insisted. "But not quite well enough to eat them."

. Johnny's fish stand was at Woodwards Cove, near Robert's factory. I was always eager for news of my fiancé. At dinner I would ask if there were any messages. Johnny had seen Robert one morning, hauling his boat onto the bank.

"How are you making out, Bob?" Johnny asked.

"Fine," Robert grunted. "I got her just where I want her."

At dinner that night, I asked Johnny if Robert had had anything to say. "Sure did," Johnny chuckled. "Bob says he's got her just where he wants her!"

My eyes widened. "Well, he doesn't want to be too sure!"

~

Castalia was about the same size as Woodwards Cove. It had two churches (the United Baptist church and the Zion Full Gospel Assembly), Johnny Graham's undertaking establishment, and a post office-store-garage run by Leon Small. Near the town, there was a natural saltwater pool that at high tide provided a perfect bathing spot.

Though I was enjoying Castalia, I was anxious to get married and set up house in Woodwards Cove. Robert had employed

Nelson Thompson to do the painting. Nelson, also a storeowner, lived right across the street. For the exterior, we chose white with black trim (the roof was green); for the interior, we chose ivory and soft pastels. Finally, all was done.

On October 27, 1928, Robert and I were married quietly in the Baptist parsonage at North Head. Lydia Dalzell and the minister's wife were our witnesses. For the occasion I wore a practical outfit— a simple brown satin dress and a blue cloth coat whose collar, cuffs, and skirt had grey fur trim. We had neither party nor honeymoon, for the herring were running, and Robert had no time for luxuries. (When the fish were in, Robert was up most of the night emptying his weirs. He'd snatch a bite of breakfast, and then he'd be off to the factory for a full day's work.)

Before couples went to the altar, they usually met with the minister performing the service. Two young people about to tie the knot had the same last names. To make sure they were not related, the minister asked them quietly, "Is there any connection?"

The groom-to-be blushed but replied honestly, "Why, yes, Reverend, once in the woodshed and twice in the barn."

This particular minister often chuckled discreetly over the failings of some of his flock. One afternoon he dropped in to see a neighbour of Uncle Willie's, a widow who was a bit of a snob. As the minister's car pulled away, Uncle Willie called out, "Had a visitor, woman?"

"Yes, that was the minister. He prayed with me."

"Played with you, did he?" asked the old man, who was going a little deaf.

"No, no, you devil. He PRAYED with me! I hope you just die."

"Die when I've a mind to, neighbour, die when I've a mind to." Uncle Willie went back indoors.

~

Our house was spacious, with living room, dining room, kitchen, and four bright bedrooms. My favourite room was the dining room, which had a large bay window overlooking the harbour. Each room was beautifully furnished, especially the master bedroom, which had a handsome bed, a large dresser, a huge chest of drawers, and a vanity with three plate-glass mirrors, one of my most prized possessions.

Whenever I look at that vanity with its mirrors, I think of Neil Tatton of Castalia, Anita Small of Woodwards Cove, and Aunt Jennie Lambert of North Head. Here's why.

Neil was a tall, slim fellow with a deadly sense of humour. One day while shaving, he took a good look at himself in the mirror.

"Neil Tatton," he proclaimed, "you're thin." Later, on his way to Woodwards Cove, he passed by Anita, who was even thinner. Next morning, as he was shaving again, Neil looked at himself in the mirror and chuckled. "I was wrong, Neil Tatton. You're fat!"

Aunt Jennie told the funniest mirror story at a senior citizen's meeting; she was eighty years old by then.

An old farmer was ploughing his fields one morning. All of a sudden the blades of his plough turned up a piece of mirror. Now, he had never seen one before, so he was quite excited.

When he looked into it, he exclaimed, "My, my! There's me old, old father!" He took the mirror home and put it in a dresser drawer. Every once in a while he'd go upstairs and gaze into the mirror. He really couldn't understand it.

His wife found his behaviour strange, so she decided to watch. She was more than a little jealous, for she suspected that her old man had another woman. Perhaps there was a letter from her in his room. She saw him gazing at something in his hand but couldn't make out what it was. She waited until he left the house, went upstairs, opened the drawer, found the mirror, and peered into it. "Ah ha!" she cried. "I knew there was another woman, and ain't she an old hag!"

~

In our new home we had a box telephone, the crude kind attached to a wall, with a crank on the side. A local telephone company had been set up on Grand Manan before I arrived, but service was confined to the island. To communicate with the mainland, you had to call Bob Parker at North Head, who then sent a telegraph to New Brunswick.

To call someone on the island, you had to turn the crank vigorously. This put you in touch with Central, and more often than not, the warm, friendly voice of Nookie Travis came through the receiver: "Hello, how are you?" (Much more inviting than the cold, nasal voices of Bell Telephone operators.)

Until the island company was sold in the fifties to the provincial network, which installed dial phones, Nookie faithfully operated the switchboard at Castalia. Of course, the system had drawbacks—there were only party lines—but it also had good points. When a fire broke out, for instance, and someone called Central, Nookie opened all the lines on the switchboard and rang everyone's number. People then raced to the scene with buckets and fire extinguishers and volunteered their services. After World War II a fire station, serviced by volunteers, was opened at Grand Harbour. But no longer did Grand Manan have Nookie Travis. Instead you had to phone the volunteer in your village, and he spread the word as quickly as possible.

Nookie provided islanders with another set of eyes. Our home had a pump in the pantry to bring up water. It broke one afternoon, so I called Elmer Wilcox of Deep Cove, electrician and plumber. No answer. I rang Central again to see if Nookie knew where Elmer was working. In minutes she phoned back and reported that Elmer was just leaving Castalia School. "If you hurry, Ina, you can catch him," she said. I grabbed a sweater, ran out to the main road, and, sure enough, along came Elmer. Before you could say "Jack Robinson," our pump was working.

By local standards Robert and I were fairly well off. But you must remember that although we had nice furniture and a car, we did not have luxuries such as vacuum cleaners, electric stoves, kettles, and refrigerators. Nobody did. We washed clothes and pumped water by hand; we cooked and heated with wood; we listened to battery-operated radios; we cut grass with hand scythes; and we read by the light of our coal-oil lamps. Those lamps had wicks that had to be trimmed, chimneys that had to be cleaned, and bowls that had to be filled. A few luckier homes, such as ours, had pressurized Coleman lamps as well; they cast an effective white light.

The first power plant was opened at Grand Harbour in 1929, just before Christmas. Money was scarce, so not many homes had this service initially. As well, it took some time to wire the houses. In the beginning the power was turned on from six in the evening until midnight. Six years later full-time service was provided, and people began to wire their houses and buy appliances. This put a great strain on the plant, and there were many power outages. Soon the plant was enlarged, but there were still breakdowns.

Just before a power interruption the lights would flicker, and Robert would look at me and say, "Now you have it, now you don't." Then ... blackness, and we'd rummage around for the kerosene and Coleman lamps. In the sixties a new generating plant was built, at Ingalls Head. But Robert and I hung on to our old Coleman lamp just in case.

~

The first years of our marriage were among the happiest of my life. I continued teaching at Castalia for a little more than a year after our wedding, so things were a little hectic, what with Robert's running the factory—Walter had started fishing full time—and my preparing lessons.

Nonetheless, I found time to manage the household affairs as well, trying my hand at Grand Manan culinary fare. At that time a lot of produce was brought right to the door. Every Friday, Friday Parker of Castalia drove up and down the island, bringing with him a broad assortment of smoked and fresh fish. His prices would be unthinkable today—he charged about twenty-five cents for a skinned haddock. Friday retired in the late thirties, but the man who took over his business sold only to hotels.

I bought our eggs from neighbours who raised hens, and I purchased our meat from Arthur Richardson, the school secretary at Castalia. He was a butcher, and he also delivered, offering fresh beef and sometimes fresh pork and spring lamb (on the outer islands, some people kept sheep). I also bought local milk products, as there was a milk co-operative. Then Robert's cousin Oscar Small opened a dairy, but the enterprise soon folded. Thereafter the refrigerated trucks of Baxter's Dairy of Saint John became a familiar sight.

Robert and I never lacked things to do. Besides movies and socials, there was baseball, tennis and, eventually, curling. There were a number of ball teams on Grand Manan, as well as several diamonds. Robert sponsored the Woodwards Cove club, whose players wore white T-shirts with his name emblazoned on them. The most convenient playing field was at Castalia, next to the community hall, and on Saturday nights, there was always a game in progress. Unusual hazards at this diamond made playing a little tricky—officials had to rig up a special fence made of tall wooden poles with fishnet draped in between. Otherwise, high flies went out to sea or landed on the rocky shelf below.

Until 1967, when a regulation pool was built, swimming was never really a popular activity. There was a sandy beach down at Deep Cove, but only the strong and the brave ventured into the nearly freezing water. The beach was an ideal spot for a picnic, though. Robert and I went there often, lighting a fire and watching the tide come in. The waves, topped with white spray, came farther and farther up the beach, and eventually our fire was doused. Then we moved on to other adventures.

One of our favourites was berrying. Wild fruits thrived all over the island. Cloudberries grew at Woodwards Cove, Ingalls Head, and on White Head Island, off the southeast coast. Known on Grand Manan as bakeapples, cloudberries are almost transparent and orange-yellow in colour. They are delicious with cream, although they do take a little getting used to.

We especially liked raspberry and blueberry expeditions. One August afternoon in 1933 Russell Bennett came with us. Russell was the brother of W.A.C. Bennett, the future premier of British Columbia, and he had married my friend Connie. That day, we found plenty of raspberries but not many blueberries. On the way home I noticed a man picking blueberries in a field. It was late, so there was no time left to pick. But I could almost taste that blueberry pie.

Robert stopped the car, and Russell and I waited while he walked over to the man and asked if he had any blueberries to sell. Eventually Robert returned with a quart. I asked him what he had paid the farmer. "One dollar," he replied.

That was exactly twice the price he should have paid. In no uncertain terms I informed my good spouse that blueberries were selling in these parts for just fifty cents a quart. Russell listened quietly to my nagging and said nothing. Later he told Connie the story, but he didn't get the name of the farmer right. Instead he gave her the name of a gentleman long dead. Knowing the island well, Connie remarked, "Well, no wonder he charged so much. Look how far he had to come to pick them!"

Bobs and Bones, Scoots and Stones

Oh my darlin' Liza Welly
Give me bread 'n' butter 'n' blueberry jelly
Then stand up, miss, 'n' give me a kiss
There's herrin' in the weir as big as yer fist

In 1928 Uncle Willie took me to the launching of the schooner *Kathleen and David* off Gaskill's Wharf at North Head. Since the late 1800s, there had been shipbuilders on Grand Manan, although there had never been a shipyard as such.

For the construction of the *Kathleen and David*, a temporary structure had been fashioned to support the schooner. Skilled craftsmen had designed and built the three-masted vessel, owned by storeowner Joseph Gaskill and named for the children of Wellington and Sadie Flagg of North Head. Island forests had provided the hackmatack and birch for the ribs for the frame, as well as the beech and maple for the planking. Lawrence Ingersoll had managed the installation of the rigging and the mechanical equipment; when readied for the sea, the schooner was put in the command of Captain Charles Gaskill.

The *Kathleen and David* was eighty-three feet long, with a twenty-foot beam and an eight-foot draft. Sadly, it was the last schooner of any size to be built on Grand Manan and, reputedly, the last three-master to be built in the Maritime provinces.

Boat building had developed hand in hand with the fishing industry. The earliest settlers, from New England, tried farming; some had stores, and a few were blacksmiths. In time, though, they realized that fishing would give them better returns. Herring were abundant, so some settlers built mud-puddle weirs, or traps, to catch them. They dug a large puddle on the shore at low tide and piled mud on the sides. When the tide came in, the fish came as well. Then when the tide went out, the fish were trapped in the puddle and scooped out. In the late 1920s the remains of a mud-puddle weir could still be found near Seal Cove.

But mud-puddle weirs didn't stand up well to the ravages of the sea. Settlers next built traps of stone, two or three feet in diameter, on rock walls. Part of one can still be seen off the shore of Nantucket Island.

When I arrived on Grand Manan, wooden weirs were the most noticeable feature. They all had names, duly recorded on each fisherman's licence. There were, to name a few, Victoria, Bluff,

Prescription, Envy, Tell-ell, Hen Clam, Try Again, Mystery, Dock, Gold King, Bread 'n' Butter, Turnip Patch, and even Toe Jam.

Weirs are circular in shape, with an opening at one end for herring to enter. In the mid-twenties some fishermen used heavy mauls to build the supports for their weirs, driving about one hundred long wooden poles into the seabed. Others used crude pile drivers. Four to six men hoisted a heavy hardwood maul into the air by pulley. They set each stake, held firm between shears, in place and then let go of the rope attached to the maul. Down came the driver, hammering the stakes into the ocean floor. In time pile drivers were operated by gasoline engines, which made weir construction much easier.

Once the stakes were firmly in place, the fishermen nailed birch ribbons to them horizontally and, in turn, birch brush vertically to the ribbons, to form a net. In the thirties cotton twine replaced brush and ribbon, and in the mid-fifties nylon netting came into use. With every improvement, expenses rose. At first a good weir cost about two thousand dollars, not including labour. With the use of nylon netting, the cost increased tenfold.

One of my most vivid memories of early weir fishing is of a bargelike boat loaded with stakes and brush docking at the breakwater in Woodwards Cove. The name of the boat was *Jean K.;* the name of its captain, Molly Cool. In her thirties, Molly had been raised on the sea, her father a captain before her. Tall, big-boned, and mannish, she could handle a boat with the best of them.

Few women at Woodwards Cove associated with Molly. As Will Cronk would say, she was a "dungaree doll," and, what's worse, she smoked a pipe. This horrified me, especially when I saw her and Robert chatting on the wharf, laughing and exchanging tobacco pouches. Molly's speech was as salty as the sea, and she probably preferred a noggin of rum to a cup of tea any day.

~

The herring season runs from June to November, with fish entering the weirs at high tide. In the early days fishermen knew when the weirs had done the job: gulls hovered overhead and lit on the stakes. Then they went out to the weirs at low tide, gathered the fish with a seine, and put them in the hold of the boat. When the boat reached shore, one man, wearing hip waders, scooped the fish into barrels that were taken by wheelbarrow to a nearby shed. There the catch was dumped into tanks and salted. Just after World War I, Grand Harbour fisherman Lawson Wilcox designed the first sluice to pump herring into the tanks; Robert was using a sluice by the mid-twenties.

Turn-of-the-century herring stringers take a break. Good stringers could hang up to twelve thousand fish a day.

The day after the herring were put into tanks, they were stirred, to loosen the salt. The third day, they were ready for stringing. A dozen or so men, women, and children stood by at long tables, each with pointed sticks about one inch in diameter and five feet in length. They thrust the fish onto the sticks through the gills and mouth. But they had to be careful because it's easy to break the gills. Damaged herring could fall off during smoking.

Sticks were supplied in bundles of one hundred, and each time the supply was replenished, the stringer got a ticket to put in a record box nailed to the wall by each table. Stringers were paid according to the number of tickets they received. In the twenties, the pay was 25 cents per one hundred sticks; over the years, the amount rose to $1.50. As a good stringer could hang up to six hundred sticks, or about twelve thousand herring, the average daily wage was about $9.00. Today, a stringer makes $4.50 a bundle.

After the herring were strung and the sticks hung on wooden "herring horses," they went to the smokehouse. Early smoke-houses looked like rectangular barns, with vents on each side. Large sliding doors at the front were left open in the daytime to let the air circulate. Long wooden poles held them shut at night, to keep out fog and moisture; the roofs had covered vents to let out excess smoke.

The fires were built mostly with saltwater driftwood, and sawdust was added to generate smoke, as well as heat. They were kindled in little piles directly on the floor, made of gravel. The upper part of the smokehouse had long horizontal "bays," or slats, for hanging the herring. After a few days the smoke tender moved the fish from the bays to the top of the building, where they stayed until completely cured.

Smoked herring were either packed neatly in boxes lined with wax paper and sold right away, or they were sent to the boning shed for another operation. The floors of the boning sheds were covered with sawdust to absorb the oil from the herring. A number of women sat on high stools at long tables. Each woman had a pair of scissors to snip off the heads, tails, and bellies of the fish. Called "scoots," these remains were dumped into an empty basket and sold for lobster bait or fertilizer. Smell? I'll say!

Back at the tables the women continued their work. They wiggled each fish, split it open along the belly with a sharp knife, removed the backbone and the insides, and scraped off the skin. More scoots. The boneless herring were wrapped in wax paper and packed into ten- or eighteen-pound boxes. If there was a demand for specialty packs for liquor parlours, they were put into cello-

Weirs were the most noticeable feature of the island when I arrived.

phane bags. As each box or packet was filled, the women received a ticket, and, as with stringing, they were paid according to the number of tickets they earned.

When herring boxes were ready for shipping, a fisheries inspector spot-checked several at random. If he approved them, he stamped each box with the manufacturer's name and brand. For example, the output from Robert's factory was clearly stencilled with "FACTORY OF ROBERT M. SMALL, WOODWARDS COVE, CANADA," and was then shipped to a distributor, Sherman Denbow, in Lubec. Grand Manan herring was sold mainly to the United States, the West Indies, the Carolines, and other southern islands.

In the 1920s, there were some 300 smokehouses on Grand Manan, owned by about 120 independent producers. They took the output of about 100 weirs and employed nearly 1,000 people. The total investment in the industry in those days amounted to more than three quarters of a million dollars.

In the evenings I did the books for Robert by the light of our Coleman lamp. His factory employed some forty people and took herring from a number of weirs, including a handful of his own. Herring catches were purchased on a first-come-first-serve basis. The money started to go out in May or June, and there were no returns until December or January. Then, as Robert used to say, the money went out as fast as it came in, to pay the bills.

In addition to Robert and his brother, Walter, there were many successful fishermen and factory owners on Grand Manan, including Ted Griffin of North Head and the McLaughlin brothers of

Seal Cove. Of course, there is such a thing as family tradition: Robert's nephew Burton Small is one of the top fishermen today.

But there was only one king of the seas, Frank Ingersoll, Jr. His father, Frank Ingersoll, Sr., and his uncles Turner and Adian had owned Long Island, off Castalia shore. About the turn of the century, they had built two fine homes and several productive weirs. Then Frank senior bought out Turner and Adian, who moved to Grand Manan. In the early twenties Frank junior built a store, a wharf, and several new weirs on Long Island and became known as The King of Fishermen. Old Frank himself had moved to North Head and built a large home on a hill, with a cement walk leading up to the front door. In time Frank junior followed suit, and his brothers, Harley and Harry, took over the business.

~

The Depression was hard on fishermen, stringers, and factory owners alike. In 1930 one fisherman, Frank Lakeman, struck it rich, making seventeen thousand dollars. With his money, he bought a diesel generator for electricity and installed a bathroom, a real luxury. The following year he was broke. The market for herring had started to crash. The pay for stringing herring went down to ten cents for each bundle of sticks, and I can clearly remember Robert, in 1932, carting all his boxed herring to a nearby field and dumping them.

The slump in the fishing industry affected the entire island. Storekeepers suffered in particular because customers were forced to buy goods on credit. Colin Small of Castalia was the poor master, and he advanced minimal sums to the storekeepers so they could keep creditors at bay. The money came from church groups and the odd provincial government grant.

In 1935, under the direction of Conservative MLA Scott Guptill, fishermen organized a marketing board; Jake Zatzman, of McCormack and Zatzman Fisheries in Saint John, was the buyer. When an order for herring came in, allotments were given out so each producer could sell a little. By World War II the market had picked up again, and herring were selling for fifty dollars a hogshead; it was nothing to make five thousand dollars in one tide.

~

The lobsters caught in the Bay of Fundy are among the best in the world. In the nineteenth century they were so plentiful on Grand Manan that farmers picked them up along the shores at low tide and hauled them away by the cartload. They even spread them, alive, on their fields as fertilizer. Of course, they ate and canned

A boat speeds out of the wharf at Ingalls Head, where lobster fishermen congregate every November to await the opening of the season.

and sold some, too. About 1880, lobsters sold for five cents apiece, regardless of size.

In later years lobster fishing had all the markings of a race. Loaded with traps and buoys, boats congregated at Ingalls Head and Seal Cove on November 15. The wharves were piled high with extra traps and other gear. With engines racing, the fishermen waited for the season to open. The fisheries officer looked about, glanced at his watch, and at the fatal hour, eight in the morning, raised his signal gun and fired into the air. The boats sped out to sea, every fisherman hoping for fair weather as he cast his traps over the side of the boat. Once those traps were set, it was back to the jetties for another load. This annual performance continues to this day on the second Tuesday of November. Now, however, the season opens at seven, and the officer uses a whistle, not a gun.

Sometimes fishermen went out several miles to set their traps, originally weighted with flat stones and marked with white or green or amber glass floats. The first days of the season were generally the best, but more often than not a storm would come up, break the traps' moorings, and shatter the traps on the rocky bottom.

The catch was taken to the buyers at Ingalls Head and Seal Cove. Their offices were in small buildings on "lobster cars," or rafts, where they counted and weighed each lot. They stored the lobsters in sectional areas beneath the boards of the cars. Later the lobsters were put in crates, each holding approximately one hundred pounds, and taken to pounds located at Ingalls Head, Woodwards Cove, Seal Cove, and the end of the Thoroughfare Road. Eventually the lobsters made their way to market, sometimes shipped fresh but always given priority on the ferry.

In a good year a lobster fisherman could make between ten and twelve thousand dollars; out of this, of course, he had to pay for licences, bait, traps, floats, boats, crew, and repairs. Some of the well-known lobster fishermen on Grand Manan were the Cooks of Seal Cove and the Greens of Ingalls Head.

Friends used to give Robert and me plenty of lobsters, both large, the "counters," and small, the "bobs." The bobs were by far the tastiest, as good as tender chicken. The counters, on the other hand, with their coarse meat, were more like tough old hen. Lobsters were, and are, protected by conservation laws—fishermen were allowed to keep only the counters; they had to put the bobs back into the sea.

Not everyone obeyed those laws. Woodwards Cove, though, had its own self-appointed conservation officer—Uncle Willie. The village's minister, whom everyone loved and respected, was given the odd mess of bobs. He told us that God had meant them as food, so he enjoyed them thoroughly, the same as everyone else.

Uncle Willie did not agree with the minister at all. He told the reverend straight out that it was a sin to eat small lobsters, even if he didn't catch them himself. Some time later the minister met Uncle Willie on the road. The old man was carrying a bucket full of clams and was on his way home to make a nice clam pie. It was June, but Grand Mananers were permitted to dig clams only from September to April, during the months that had an *r* in their name.

"My friend," said the minister, "you know that it is unlawful to dig clams at this time of year. Is that not a sin?"

"Not goin' to sell these, Reverend," Uncle Willie said. "Just a few to eat, just a few to eat."

~

Besides herring and lobster, groundfish have always been plentiful. Early settlers used handlines and, by the 1850s, gillnets. Today many fish for cod, halibut, and pollock. They also drag for scallops. In the twenties this was done by hand with a metal-framed bag. At that time scallops were shocked, or the meat removed, onshore and the shells cast aside. Islanders collected the shells and used them for ashtrays or cooking utensils, or painted scenes in the interior and mounted them on small stands.

At the end of every fishing season, in November, the men spread their nets and seines in fields to dry. One field in Woodwards Cove was owned by a blind woman. One time, during the Depression, she ran out of her house as the fishermen were spreading their nets and blasted them for tearing up her field.

The field was not in use at the time, so the fishermen told her to go away and mind her own business. Furious, the woman called the police. The one and only RCMP constable, R.K. Ackman, arrived on the scene, but he just smiled at the woman and said, "You know, madame, for a person who is drawing the blind pension, you sure do see a lot."

~

Despite the broad range of seafood in Fundy waters, Grand Mananers have always been particular about their fish. Scallops dipped in cornmeal and fried in butter, boneless herring baked in a little water, pollock cakes and hash, and fried halibut were favourite dishes. But few islanders chose cod, and many cast mackerel aside. Mackerel came in with herring, only to be dumped in separate barrels. Children often went to the wharves, grabbed some mackerel, and sold them door to door for pocket money. At first I was cautious about trying the dark, oily meat, but I soon acquired a taste for it.

Not so tuna. When I was teaching at Woodwards Cove, someone caught a huge tuna and parked it near the road. All the villagers were excited—free food and even some to can. People chopped off sizable chunks of meat, whatever they wanted. The flesh was so red that it reminded me of horse meat. The sight of that large bloody carcass, all hacked to bits, put me off tuna for life. Shortly after, I saw my first whale, lying on the shore. It had been trapped in a weir, and some fishermen had hauled it onto the beach. Needless to say, I didn't hang around to see what happened to that carcass.

A Lighthouse for Evelyn

Could we but know the grief they felt
As the Exile drifted into space,
And as in prayer that night they knelt,
Grim death unveiled its hideous face.
—Archer Coy Wilcox

In all, there are a handful of lighthouses and fog alarms on the shores of Grand Manan and on the surrounding islands. The first lighthouses were built in the 1830s on Gannet Rock and Machias Seal Island, about five miles off the south shore. Over the years, they have been serviced by various supply boats. From 1920 to 1955, the *Franklin* delivered supplies to the lighthouses; until 1980, the *Walter G. Foster* carried that responsibility; today, helicopters fulfil the need.

The Machias Seal and Gannet lights mark each side of the Murr Ledges, the death trap for many a fine ship. The lighthouse on Gannet Rock, named for the large-billed birds, has been seen on clear nights from Saint John, some forty-five miles away. Before the 1950s, there were always two keepers on that island, isolated for months at a time. Only one wedding has ever taken place on Gannet: Esther and Henry MacDonald's on May 15, 1854. Esther was the sister of the lighthouse keeper, Walter McLaughlin, who served for about thirty years.

The next lighthouse, Swallowtail, was built at North Head. Wilfrid Dalzell, an old friend of mine, was the first baby born at Swallowtail, on the eve of April 3, 1894, a snowy, stormy night. A woodcarver in his spare time, Wilfrid joined the army during World War I and then moved to the mainland, living in St. Andrews and then in Saint John. He died in 1973 and was buried in the Anglican Church of the Ascension Cemetery, near the place of his birth.

In the early 1870s The Whistle was opened at Long Eddy, on the northernmost tip of Grand Manan. Here the tides from the Atlantic and the Bay of Fundy seem to meet, creating a swell known as The Rips. In a storm, it is said, this can be the roughest stretch of water in the world.

About five years later lighthouses were established at Fish Fluke Point, on the eastern coast of Ross Island, and at Southern Head, at the bottom of Grand Manan. The old lighthouse at Southern Head—there is a new one now—was large and contained

The waters get rough around Swallowtail Light, one of the unmarked gravestones for the sailors and fishermen who have perished at sea.

living quarters for the keeper. Before I was married, I walked around the head of the cliffs and farther along the shore, getting a glimpse of the natural rock formation the Southern Cross.

Lighthouse and fog-alarm construction continued. A fog alarm was built on Big Duck Island in 1887, and in the first part of the twentieth century, Gull Cove Light and the Long Point alarm, both on White Head Island, were established.

~

For me the lighthouses stand as testimonies to the unpredictable weather—the dense fog, the howling gales, the heavy rains. They are the gravestones of all the sailors and fishermen who have been lost at sea. I can't begin to recount all the ships that have been eaten up by the ocean, but museum curator Eric Allaby has charted the shipwrecks in the area. It is a sobering document.

One of the most engaging stories comes from an epic poem by Archer Coy Wilcox, "Flight of the *Exile*," published in 1976. The *Exile*, a 112-ton brigantine, was built at Deep Cove in 1838 by Charles Dyer Wilcox; Nelson Card was master. In the fall of 1846 she sailed from Pictou, Nova Scotia, bound for New York. A few miles off Cape Sable Island she encountered a gale that blew for more than a week. The storm had struck without warning—many of the crew were drowned, and parts of the vessel were blown away. In nine days the storm drove the *Exile* halfway across the Atlantic. Card lightened ship to keep her from foundering, but the food supplies were nearly exhausted, the survivors living on hard tack and water. On New Year's Eve the *Exile* reached Crookhaven, Ireland. Card sold the boat, and one crew member, William Wilcox, met and married a miller's daughter.

Meanwhile, debris from the brigantine was found in Maritime waters. It was believed that the *Exile* and all aboard had perished. Sorrow struck the homes of Grand Manan, and a memorial service was held. Fourteen months after he had left Pictou, however, William Wilcox and his bride walked into his father Charles Dyer's home and handed over the money from the sale of the *Exile*.

~

Whenever I neared the 150-foot cliff Ashburton Head, just east of The Whistle, I thought of the cliff's namesake, the *Lord Ashburton*. Fully rigged, with a crew of twenty-seven, the ship crashed into the head on a stormy and foggy night in January 1857. Most of the crew huddled together for warmth, but seven men plunged into the icy waters and swam ashore. One sailor, James Lawson, managed to climb the cliff in his bare feet.

*I caught a glimpse of the natural rock formation the Southern Cross in
1927. The ravages of weather and tides have since washed it away.*

A North Head resident, James Tatton, was out walking, and he
noticed bloody footprints in the snow. He followed the tracks to an
old barn where he found Lawson barely alive. Lawson was able to
mutter the words "wreck ... men ... help them." But only seven of
the crew had survived. Lawson remained on Grand Manan and
later raised money for a monument in the North Head cemetery.
He became a shoemaker, painting watercolours of the sea and
rocks in his spare time.

When ships were wrecked, islanders turned into scavengers,
even Robert and I. In 1909 the steamer *Hestia* hit the Old
Proprietor Ledge, northeast of Gannet Rock. Sadly, thirty-five
people lost their lives. The ship was also carrying whiskey galore,
and barrels of the spirit floated around the island for weeks. Many
Grand Mananers gave in to their baser instincts and salvaged
much of the cargo for "medicinal purposes." On another occasion,
decades later, there was a minor shipwreck off the east coast. No
one was killed, but the coal-laden vessel spewed its cargo all over
the rocks. I have vague recollections of surreptitious nocturnal
outings, of blinking car headlights and of small boats rowing to the

scene. Fortune favoured those midnight mariners ... Robert and I had coal to burn for more than a year.

～

There probably isn't a single soul on Grand Manan who hasn't been personally affected by a tragedy at sea. Before 1926 Bud and Irene Lyons, other strangers from away, moved to Grand Manan from New York. They had four children: Howard, 15, Bonny, 13, Evelyn, 7, and Guy, 5. I knew the three older children because they came to school to me at Castalia. Howard and Bonny were pleasant boys, but Evelyn was irresistible, with her dark hair and sunny disposition. I can still picture Evelyn walking into school in September 1928, holding her mother's hand.

Bud had taken up lobster fishing, but he had little knowledge of the sea. The flood tides in the Bay of Fundy are the highest in the world, rising to about thirty feet, hiding treacherous ledges. The boys of Grand Manan are raised on the ocean. They know the ebbs of the tides, they know the areas to avoid, they know the narrow, shallow passages.

In the early spring of 1932 Bud set his traps. The tides were high—at Woodwards Cove we couldn't even drive to the breakwater. On April 30, a fine sunny day, Bud decided to check his catch; Howard, Guy, and Evelyn went with him. Everything went smoothly, but on the journey home disaster struck.

Near shore the boat hit a rock that ripped away part of its bottom. Bud took Evelyn on his back, Howard took Guy, and they jumped into the water. The sea was so cold that neither Howard nor Bud was able to swim to shore. Instead they hung on to the rock, praying for a rescue party. Eventually Evelyn said, "Daddy, I can't hold on any longer." Bud tried to encourage her, but she let go and sank into the water. Shortly Guy let go as well. At last a boat did pick up Bud and Howard, exhausted and speechless with grief.

I was standing at my kitchen window when I noticed a crowd gathering at a neighbour's shed. I saw men carrying one body, then another. They slid Bud and Howard into the back of a car, but the doors were left open because they were unable to bend their legs.

Bud and Howard were driven home and put to bed. Bud was hysterical and blamed himself for the tragedy. A search for the bodies of Evelyn and Guy got under way immediately. Unequipped with lights, the boats had to stop looking as night fell. At dawn a whole fleet gathered, but with the changing of the tides, no one was sure where to begin. The boats covered a vast area. Finally, almost on the verge of giving up, Robert's brother, Walter, struck something with an oar. He had found the bodies.

The children were only a few hundred yards from shore. Although they had gone down separately, their arms were wrapped tightly around each other. It was a gruesome sight, as their faces had been eaten away by sea fleas, no respectors of persons. They were taken to Johnny Graham's undertaking establishment in Castalia for a closed-casket service.

Bud gave up fishing, and in a few years he, Irene, and Bonny left Grand Manan; Howard remained and married Johnny Graham's daughter, Lorena. Howard, too, died at an early age, leaving a son, Tony.

For years Bud Lyons had followed the same old routine. Going to and from his traps, he passed that rock every time. It was called Buck's Rock and was located between Woodwards Cove and Grand Harbour. He had always missed it, but he had been heard to say, "Darn that rock. Someday it's going to get me."

~

Never a Dull Moment

With our apricots, onions, and apples ...
Eggplant and lime for latrines
We're the greatest of all country grocers
With the best store you've ever seen

Nearly everyone on Grand Manan had a vegetable garden. In particular, Uncle Willie's was lush and large. But one summer someone kept stealing his produce. To deter the guilty party, the old man put up a sign that read, "You were here last night! If you're here tonight, you'll still be here in the morning!" Most people knew Uncle Willie kept a shotgun, but few knew it was rarely loaded. "The sign worked, Ina," Uncle Willie chuckled. "That thief never came back."

As the old man was recounting his most recent victory, there was the faint, distant sound of a truck horn. Uncle Willie took out his pocket watch. "That'd be Rue Ingalls, right on time as usual." In a moment Rue came into view, his old truck rattling along at a fast clip. Rue gave another lusty blast of his horn and thundered past in a cloud of dust. Uncle Willie took out his watch again. "Well, mebbe Rue's running a little late today."

Rue Ingalls late? Impossible! Rue was born in 1894 at Southern Head Light; his grandfather, Walter McLaughlin, who had left Gannet Rock in the 1880s, was the lightkeeper. Rue started to carry the mail in 1912, when he was just eighteen. In those days he drove a buckboard in summer, a sleigh in winter. He got the mail through despite storms or accidents, and one winter, he told me, the snow was so deep you could sit on the telephone wires.

In 1917 Rue gave up the mail contract and started a hauling business. But he took on the job again in 1932, driving his old truck, which looked like an old-fashioned stagecoach. On one trip the kingbolt broke, and Rue tumbled out of the truck head first. He managed to get to Grand Harbour, where he woke up Albert Harvey, the blacksmith. It was five in the morning, but Albert forged a new kingbolt for Rue, and the mail got through. On another trip the truck just died. Rue left it and borrowed two horses, riding one and slinging the mailbags over the back of the other.

As Rue delivered the mail down the island, he'd often see a storm coming. Immediately he'd turn around, retrace his route, and pick up the outgoing mail ahead of the blizzard so the mail wouldn't

Men used to gather in village stores and exchange stories. Their wives, of course, thought that this was terrible, but they were quick to ask about all the gossip when their husbands came home.

miss the morning ferry. In winter Rue's job was often made easier by men and boys who shovelled the snow in lieu of paying taxes. (These people worked just as hard in summer, clearing the roadsides of alders and other small trees. In later years government employees took over this task, but they never bothered to clear the roads until late fall. As time went by, the roadways were littered with beer cans, bottles, paper, and food containers.)

Soon Rue had a proper half-ton truck that was boxed in at the back. The winter storms didn't change, though. During one dreadful blow, he only got as far as Castalia, where he went over the bank. But this did not stop Rue. In the grand old tradition of His Majesty's Mail he commandeered a rowboat, carried down the mailbags, slung them aboard, and rowed for one and a half hours to catch the steamer, which left at seven in the morning.

Rue carried letters and parcels of all shapes and sizes. Some Grand Mananers did mail-order shopping, and for many the Eaton's catalogue was a book of wonders. Now and then, though, the company did make mistakes. One time a Woodwards Cove woman, Annie Brown, had sent for a blue suit. When Rue delivered the parcel, she opened it and found a green one. She gave Rue a snappy letter of complaint to mail: "If you knew how hard I had to skin [herring] to get that money, you'd have sent me what I ordered. Green ain't blue, and blue ain't green!"

Rue retired in 1973. He had driven more than 360,000 miles and had owned fifteen trucks in all. Over the years one of his regular stops had been the Draper establishment at Woodwards Cove. Now, Pete and Alice Draper lived above the business; out back they had a small farm. Pete hated to get up early and let Rue in to collect the mail. So Rue would pull up outside and blow his horn loud and long. Pete would get out of bed, open the upstairs window, and throw down the mail. By the time Rue was on his way, Pete would be back in bed, warm and snug for another few hours' shuteye.

~

The Draper place was legendary. As at the other stores in Woodwards Cove, and on the rest of the island, for that matter, people liked to congregate there, find out the news, and have a good chinwag. The ladies didn't approve, of course. They'd go in and out of the store briskly, leaving their husbands behind. But when the men returned home, the women were just as quick to ask about all the latest gossip.

The stories that flowed from the Drapers' were among the most incredible tales ever heard. One day a fisherman was bragging about how fast he could run. He said he had been out picking blueberries on the mainland when all of a sudden a bear had started to chase him. He had run so hard that he had finally come to a frozen lake. He had managed to get across it safely. The bear, on the other hand, had fallen through the ice, so the fisherman had escaped.

"Hold on there," cried Pete. "I thought you said it was berrying season. Lakes don't freeze then.

"It was," replied the braggart. "But I had to run till Christmas to get away from that bear!"

When Alice was on duty, things were never dull. She had a reputation for being somewhat prim and proper, but it was sullied one afternoon by a remark she made. It happened while Pete was busy in the field stacking hay into haycocks, ready for loading and hauling into the barn. "Where's Pete?" asked Rue as he delivered a sack of mail.

"Pete's up in the field, doodling up his 'cock," Alice replied. For once Rue was speechless.

Alice had a reputation for being nosy, too. She often called out loudly to passers-by. "Hey, fellow," she once yelled to a neighbour driving by in his wagon, "what are you haulin' today?"

With relish, the man yelled, "Why, Alice, I'm haulin' shee-it!"

In Castalia, there was a set of identical twins, Gleason and Gracon Winchester. One of them liked to chew tobacco, and he bought his chaws at the Drapers' store, but he always ordered just one cent worth. Chew came in figs, so this meant cutting off a tiny chunk each time. Alice, not known for mincing words, either, finally got a little tired of all this effort for such a small sale.

"Why don't you take the whole fig?" she asked in some exasperation. Her customer popped the tobacco into his mouth and chewed for several moments before replying, "Too much terbacca ta chew, Alice, too much terbacca ta chew."

Pete was no slouch behind the counter, either. "Ina, I swear he's the best salesman on God's green earth," Uncle Willie told me one day. "Just last week, widow Smith went into the post office to buy a suit of clothes to bury her husband in. Pete sold her a brand new suit with two pairs of pants!"

More than anything else, the Drapers were kind, often helping their customers when they ran short of money. Uncle Willie had a first-rate reputation for paying his bills promptly, so when he needed some things in a hurry, he had no trouble getting a little credit from Pete.

In the winter of 1935 Uncle Willie was having a particularly hard time making ends meet. He went to the Drapers' to get some groceries on credit, and since Pete knew that Uncle Willie's pension cheque was due soon, Pete gladly gave the old man what he needed.

A few days later, there was a terrible snowstorm. The place was deserted. Pete looked at Alice. "Let's close up shop early and go upstairs. There won't be anyone around here tonight." So they turned out all the lights and went up to their apartment. Outside, the wind howled and whistled around the old frame building, and the snow drifted across the road. At the height of the storm, there was a sudden frantic knocking on the door. It was nearly midnight. Pete groaned, crawled out of his warm bed, made his way downstairs, and turned on the lights. In the doorway stood a snow-covered figure he barely recognized. "Uncle Willie! What on earth are you doing out this terrible night?"

"Came to pay my bill. Said I would soon as my cheque came. Hasn't come yet, but my cousin arrived—paid off a little debt—so here," said the old man, handing over a dollar bill and a bit of change.

"Come on in, Uncle Willie, and get warm." Pete shivered in the open doorway as the wind whirled up his nightshirt.

"No, thank you. Got a couple o' other bills ta pay. Me and Sal'll be on our way." The old man got into his cutter, and he and his faithful mare disappeared into the whirling snow, with a merry jingle of sleigh bells. "G'night, Pete," he called, his credit rating restored and his conscience cleared. Pete looked at the money in his hand and shook his head. Snug in bed once again, he said to Alice, "You know, that man really has to be my favourite customer!"

~

Pete and Alice had been married for several years when I arrived in Woodwards Cove. Alice, however, was Pete's second wife—his first wife had died. Pete was in his mid-thirties, and it was rumoured that Alice was quite a bit older.

But the course of true love is never smooth. Shortly after the Drapers purchased their first automobile, Uncle Willie dropped by just in time to see Pete scraping and washing a mess off the side of the Ford. "What's that all over yer car, Pete?"

"Gulls' eggs," Pete replied and proceeded to tell his story.

The night before, there had been a revival meeting at Seal Cove. The Drapers had decided to drive down, he to the church meeting, she to visit some friends. Pete dropped Alice off and arranged to pick her up after the revival. Now, those night-time revivals lasted late, often until after midnight. About eleven Alice realized that her friends were tired and probably wanted to go to bed. She figured that because Pete hardly ever took her anywhere in the new car, he had forgotten all about her. She would have to walk the eight miles home. As she bade her friends good night, they gave her a treat of a half-dozen gulls' eggs in a pagerbag. She set out on her journey, not in a happy frame of mind. On and on she walked. She hoped and prayed that someone would come along and give her a lift but no such luck. The farther she walked, the angrier she became.

As it turned out, Pete hadn't forgotten her. After the revival he had stopped to chat with the minister. Alice was almost in sight of the house when her husband drew alongside and called out, "Do you want a lift?" By this time Alice was hopping mad. She snatched an egg from the bag and hurled it at Pete. "I take it," he said, rolling up the window, "that you don't care to ride." Before he drove off, she had tossed the rest of the eggs at the car. A gull's egg is about three times the size of the average hen's egg, so Pete had a king-size job removing the mess the next morning.

Actually, Pete was a bit of a handyman. He had rigged up a pipe from the store to the living quarters above, with a lid on top, so customers could yell up if he or Alice were in the apartment.

Uncle Willie left Pete scrubbing the Ford and went inside. There was no one downstairs. He rapped on the pipe.

"What do you want?" came a sleepy metallic voice from above. Uncle Willie called up as loud as he could, "I was wonderin' if you had any gulls' eggs for sale?" Bang went the cover over the pipe! Alice was not amused.

Alice and Pete had two sons, eight-year-old Harold and six-year-old Mulvey. Harold always took a short cut across the fields on his way home from school. He'd slip into the henhouse to see how many eggs had been laid. No, Harold didn't collect them, he just counted them. And there was always one added attraction, a hearty set-to with the lord of the manor, a large and vicious rooster. Invariably the rooster attacked the boy, but for Harold this was high adventure.

On one particular afternoon the rooster seemed more aggressive than usual. The cheeky boy picked up a stick to defend himself. During the course of the scrimmage he gave the rooster a good whack. The bird flew out of the henhouse, neck upthrust, making an odd noise.

Harold went inside and said, "Ma, there's something wrong with your rooster. He's makin' funny noises." Alice looked at the bird and called Pete, who looked, too. Father decided he'd better kill the bird right then and there, before it died. Grabbing his axe, Pete picked up the rooster and off he went to the chopping block.

That Sunday the rooster made its final appearance, roasted to a turn. Everyone wanted to have the wishbone. "My goodness," cried Alice, carving the bird, "the wishbone is broken! I wonder how come?" Harold confessed all. In a rare moment of unanimity his fighting parents had a good laugh. As for Harold, the brave lad managed to polish off the remains of his old enemy in a most satisfying fashion.

Harold and Mulvey were always in and out of trouble. Uncle Willie called the Draper boys "incident prone." Take the night they decided to camp outdoors behind the store. They put up the family tent and dragged over enough stones to make a crude rock fireplace. It is never too warm on Grand Manan—the nights especially tend to be chilly—so the boys wanted a warm fire. But having expended their energy on tent erection and fireplace construction, they were too tired to chop wood and decided to help themselves to the freshly cut kindling in the kitchen, the kindling Pete had laid out for Alice to light the morning fire.

Pete was awakened at dawn by some especially strong language from his spouse. "Where's the kindling?" she cried. Where indeed! It didn't take Pete long to discover the ashes of a warm fire outside his sons' camp. He knew at once what had happened. So he told Alice to crawl back into bed. "I'll light the fire, my angel," he said, or words to that effect.

Quietly Pete lifted the fly of the tent. Both his sons were still sound asleep. Mulvey's arms were outstretched, and Pete gently pressed a good chunk of hen manure into each hand of the sleeping boy. Mulvey stirred slightly; Pete quickly withdrew and had the pleasure of watching his sons self-destruct.

Mulvey stretched, smelled something "fowl," and woke up with a loud holler. He reached over and wiped his hands on Harold's nightshirt. That started a grand fight and chase. Harold seized a cow plop and pelted it at Mulvey. Mulvey ran right across the field to the shore, with his brother in close pursuit. By the time it was all over, both boys were covered in dung. Pete, meanwhile, had chopped a fresh lot of kindling, boiled a kettle, and treated his startled wife to a cup of hot tea in the boudoir.

Characters

Characters all the folks you meet
Characters ... everyone's a treat
Brave Captain Kidd docked undeterred
A ship is wrecked and rum's the word
And a local gave the Yanks a bird
They're characters, everyone.

I was saddened one day by something an old acquaintance from Washington, D.C. said to me. "You know, Mrs. Small, I've been coming to Grand Manan for the past thirty years," she lamented, "but now I'm selling my cottage. Grand Manan has lost its colour. All the *real* characters are gone." She was right to some extent. Many of the truly endearing people who had once brightened the island were gone, although their vitality, their sparkle, lives on in new generations of islanders.

Few were more charming and fun loving than Dark Harbour dulsers William and Lewis Green. They were known as Darby and Lucy, the Dark Harbour Hermits, but no classification could have been further from the truth. Darby and Lucy loved to entertain the tourists, and the tourists loved to watch. Lucy's hair was long—he'd have been in style in the sixties—and he and Darby dressed in unusual costumes, claiming they could commune with spirits. They had a so-called magic box that contained small hand-carved wooden figures and an eagle flying off with an infant. Lit with flashlight bulbs, the entire interior could be seen through magnifying-lense peepholes. They also had a gun that shot out small pictures, but more entertaining still was their poetry, which they recited at the drop of a hat.

Darby and Lucy's camp was perched on top of a hill, beside a natural spring that bubbled with cold water. They had routed the water into a wooden tub that had a large nail driven through one side. A rusty old tin cup hung from the nail, and anyone who visited their humble home had to have a drink. One sunny summer afternoon a group of tourists dropped by, and being gracious, each visitor took a swig. But one rather fastidious young woman carefully turned the cup around and held it in her left hand. As she gingerly took a sip, one of the hermits remarked loudly, "Lady, I see you drink out of the same side I do!"

I first met Darby and Lucy in 1926, having found my own way to Dark Harbour, on the west coast. The old trail wound wildly over the Laboree Hill, often providing panoramic views of the rolling countryside. Near the end the road narrowed to a single track, and a warning sign proclaimed, "Go further at your own risk!" Then there was a sudden sharp curve and a spectacular drop to the bottom of the hill.

Three quarters of the dulse sold in Canada and the United States is harvested at Dark Harbour, also a nesting ground for bald eagles. This famous seaweed is rich in potassium, phosphatic salts, and iodine. Though there is some dulsing on the eastern side of Grand Manan, that harvest does not compare to the Dark Harbour product, richer in colour and flavour. In the twenties dry dulse sold for three cents a pound, and a good dulser could gather about 400 pounds of wet dulse a tide, which he then spread out on the sea wall to dry. Dulsing season ran from June to October, with the overall annual harvest totalling about 150,000 pounds.

Darby and Lucy always emerged from Dark Harbour on May 24 and July 1 to celebrate. There were ball games, special movies and dances, and big parades. And everywhere you looked, there were the hermits, right in the thick of things. Eventually, like everyone else, Darby and Lucy grew old. They left Dark Harbour and built a camp on Cedar Street in Castalia, where they lived happily till the end of their days.

~

Nowhere were tourists treated with greater hospitality than at Grand Manan hotels. In 1932 Miss Sabra Jane Briggs bought the rambling North Head home of Frank Ingersoll, Sr., father of The King of Fishermen, and turned it into a resort called The Anchorage. As the years passed and her business grew, she moved The Anchorage to the large Daggett home, near Long Pond, on the road between Grand Harbour and Seal Cove. A huge anchor and rock marked the entrance to the spacious grounds.

Sabra Jane had the wagon shed moved and attached to the main house. The shed was renovated and turned into a large rustic dining area that contained a big fieldstone fireplace and seated some sixty guests. She converted the old barn into living quarters for the staff, and she built cabins in the surrounding woods. The resort was quite primitive, with no electric lights and no radios or telephones. People who wanted a true refuge patronized the place, and there were plenty of them.

Sabra Jane gave her guests the kind of special treatment that brought them back year after year. She met them at the ferry when they arrived and took them to the ferry when they departed, bidding them farewell with her unusual cross-armed wave. Dur-

Lucy (left) and Darby, the Dark Harbour Hermits, entertained tourists at the drop of a hat.

ing their stay she drove to the Grand Harbour post office each day and picked up the mail, sorting it for her guests and placing it in separate boxes. She planned excursions around Grand Manan, as well as to Machias Seal Island and Gannet Rock. For those outings, she prepared individual box lunches wrapped in red and white cloths.

Sabra Jane took just as much interest in the wildlife. The New Brunswick government had introduced deer to the island, and whenever she saw some near her hotel, she encouraged them to come closer so her guests could see them. She fed the deer regularly, and they eventually became tame.

In 1948 Sabra Jane Briggs sold The Anchorage to Gerry and Sally l'Aventure of Toronto. They kept the Sabra Jane touch alive and even founded a bird sanctuary at Long Pond. About 1965 the New Brunswick government bought the resort and turned it into a campground.

Other special places to stay included the Marathon Hotel and Whale Cove Cottages. In the twenties "drummers," or travelling salesmen, used to stay at the Marathon, in North Head, because it was the only place open year round. Manny and Mabel Kent owned the Marathon, and they were the perfect hosts. Manny always drove the drummers down the island in a fine horse and carriage, stopping at the stores in each village.

Whale Cove Cottages, today owned by Kathleen Buckley, were well worth a visit, too. They were located near the cottage of American novelist Willa Cather, who spent summers on Grand Manan from 1922 until 1940. Her cottage, with its lovely view, was secluded and quiet, a hideaway from the rest of the world. On her death the cottage was passed to her secretary, and it became rundown, the shrubs and grounds overgrowing beyond beauty. Happily, when it was returned to the family, it was completely refurbished, becoming quite lovely again.

~

Whale Cove Cottages and Willa Cather's summer retreat were near the road to The Whistle. Endless steps led down to the old fog alarm, situated right on the shore. (In later years a lighthouse was built on top of the bank.) From The Whistle you could continue down the hill some distance until you came to a bend in the road. There was a gate leading to the Garden of Eden, the home of Wesley (Wessie) Griffin, the artist.

There was a bell at the gate. If Wessie was painting and not wanting guests, he ignored its ring. If, however, he was in the mood for a visit, he welcomed you warmly. From the gate, natural stone steps led up to the main house and studio; only poles on the outer edges kept you from falling over the embankment.

His garden was beautiful. An old pipe fed spring water into a fountain in the middle, and everywhere there were lupins, wild roses, columbine, larkspur, and ferns. Rustic seats were scattered here and there, as were poppies, nasturtiums, and other flowers. The garden was a confusion of blooms.

At each end was a rough wooden pillar. A statue of Adam stood on one; a statue of Eve on the other. At the far end of the garden, behind the guest cottage, the view was breathtaking. There was a sheer drop of three hundred feet down to the sea, and on a clear day you could see the coast of Maine and Campobello Island. To the southwest was Money Cove, where the dashing Captain Kidd reputedly stashed some of his treasure.

It was never all work and no play with Wesley Griffin. One day he heard about a barrel of rum that had washed ashore at Whale Cove. Two men had found it and knocked out the bung so any passer-by could help himself. "Lead me to it!" Wessie cried, abandoning a canvas and rushing off for a tot. In his haste to quench his thirst, he nearly fell over the enbankment. The painting was later completed—much later.

Wessie exhibited in London, New York, Paris, and Rome. He painted in the rich dark colours of the old masters, but his realist technique was his own. One of his paintings, *The Young Captain*, can be seen in the library of the high school, at Grand Harbour. It is a delightfully whimsical study of Grand Manan's maritime heritage. The "captain" of the painting, supposedly a self-portrait, is a young lad of fourteen clad in sou'wester and slicker, standing near a rowboat.

Wessie helped many island painters, and he encouraged others to take up the challenge when perhaps they never would have painted at all. I wasn't one of them, although I often observed him painting and studied his canvases. The inspiration of his work, though, was a different matter. It has never left me.

Other islanders just used to watch Wessie at work. They always wanted to know what he was painting. One time a youngster asked him, "Where is that picture?"

"What in hell does it matter?" Wessie replied. "It's a damn good picture, isn't it?"

Grand Manan has attracted other artists: Paul Berthom and Lester Stevens from the United States and Jack Humphrey, Miller Brittain, and Ted and Rosamund Campbell from mainland New Brunswick. The rocky shores and the vegetation have been favourite subjects. At Deep Cove a single alder stands on a high cliff. Called the "weather-vane" tree, it has no branches on the south side, the direction from which the wind blows. The tamaracks there lean to the east, and they, like the rest of the trees at Deep Cove, have been stunted by the salty spray of the sea.

In spring and summer, the wild flowers and blossoms offer a burst of colour that can't be matched anywhere. There are lilacs, lupins, sweet peas, morning glories, heather, and apple blossoms. In fall, there are catkins, sumach, and white maples turning yellow with a hint of orange here and there. All of Grand Manan, it seems, is a Garden of Eden.

Just as I'll never forget the beauty of Grand Manan vegetation, I'll never get over the number of birds on the island. In 1833 Audobon himself came to observe sea gulls nesting. Since then many birders have visited, some claiming to have actually sighted as many as 275 species.

But there was only one "birdman," Allan Moses, the taxidermist at North Head. Allan had influenced young Yale graduate J. Sterling Rockefeller to buy Kent Island in 1930 and set up a bird sanctuary to protect that eider-duck breeding ground. Kent Island, part of Three Islands, off the southeast shore, covers about 150 acres and has been home to up to sixty thousand gulls and thousands of petrels, as well as eider ducks, whose down has been used to make puffs for beds and to stuff pillows. When a few hours old, the eider ducklings plunge into the sea, only to return when they're ready to mate.

In 1935 Rockefeller turned the island over to Bowdoin College in Brunswick, Maine, so scholars could study its birdlife. From then on, about fifteen students visited Kent Island every summer, and in time seven buildings were erected, including a well-equipped laboratory. The young ornithologists not only examined the habits of the eider ducks, they also monitored the Leach's stormy petrels, known to islanders as Mother Carey's chickens. They tagged these birds and discovered that in the fall they migrated by night to St. George's Island in the Azores, a distance of eight thousand miles. One petrel made this journey seven times, a distance equivalent to more than twice around the world.

Year after year the petrels return to the same nest. The young birds make their own new homes, tunnelling under a bush about a yard and taking a sharp turn to the right. Here they lay their eggs, only one a year, white and fragile. Holding an egg up to the light, you can see through it, even the embryo inside. The eggs take about fifty days to hatch, with mothers and fathers taking three-

The "weather-vane" tree at Deep Cove has no branches on the south side, the direction from which the wind blows.

or four-day shifts on the nests. After the eggs hatch, seventy days pass before the young can fly. Then they emerge only when it is dark—no doubt instinct tells them that hungry gulls may be waiting for them during daylight.

Ernest Joy was guardian and resident naturalist on Kent Island for many years. From Seal Cove, he lived on Inner Wood Island. In a roundabout way it was he who had brought Allan Moses and J. Sterling Rockefeller together. Ernest had shot a yellow-nosed albatross and brought it to Allan to stuff and mount. This species was usually found south of the Equator, so Allan wrote the American Museum of Natural History about the bird. Astounded that it had been found so far north, the museum's curators asked to buy it. But Allan, who had a museum of his own, decided to keep it for his collection. Later he changed his mind and said he would trade the albatross for the privilege of going on a scientific expedition sponsored by the museum.

So it came to be that Allan accompanied J. Sterling Rockefeller and C.B.G. Murphy, another recent Yale graduate, to Tanganyika and the Belgian Congo to hunt for the rare green broadbill. Allan had contracted malaria during the expedition, and while the others were out hunting one day, he slept. He woke up and, peering out the flap of his tent, saw a bird on a nearby tree. Without hesitation, he picked up his gun and shot it. Sure enough, it was a green broadbill.

Over the years Allan's collection of mounted birds grew enormously, and in 1951 he turned it over to the students of Grand Manan. He died in 1953.

~

Islanders took a keen interest in their feathered friends, building small feeding stations everywhere. Around the shores I saw sandpipers, cranes, ducks, blue jays, yellow warblers, grosbeaks, robins, and golden-winged woodpeckers, not to mention gulls. Gulls lay their eggs in June, two or three to a nest. The eggs are tan with dark brown specks. If there were three in a nest, islanders never touched them, but if there were one or two, they took them. Then the mother laid three more.

Of course, the familiar V of Canada geese always told us when spring and winter were coming. My friend Uncle Willie claimed that the large geese allowed the small ones to perch on their backs for the long migratory flights. A wonderful thought, but Uncle Willie always was an incurable romantic.

One bird I do not miss is the swallow. Our house was constantly pestered by those stubborn birds. There were many old sheds around the shore, but would the swallows build their nests on those? Never. They preferred our home. Robert and I had a sheltered spot on the southeast corner of our verandah, and that is where the pesky birds built their nests year in, year out.

One summer I took my broom and knocked down a nest—no big thing. But the birds came back. In the afternoon I knocked the nest down again. They came back again, this time with all their relations. Then I swung my broom at them to frighten them from their work. The nerve of those swallows! They dove right at me, swooping so vindictively that I left them to it.

Early the following morning I swept the half-finished nest down again and washed off all the mud. Then I tacked up a large plastic bag where the nest had been. That did it. The swallows left us alone—until the next summer.

Starlings were wily, too, stealing nests from birdhouses. Uncle Willie had a method of dealing with those thieves. One summer he hung a dead starling outside his birdhouse, wrapping a single hair from old Sal's tail around its neck. He claimed that this acted as a warning.

"Did the starlings stay away, Uncle Willie?"

"You're damn right they did, Ina," he chuckled, lighting his pipe and puffing away triumphantly.

A Dedicated Doctor
and a Consolidated High School

Oh, how I longed to be a doctor
And treat the world for its ills
How mighty quick I'd heal the sick
With paregorics and pills

On July 26, 1931, Robert and I were blessed with a daughter, Maureen. She was my little sweetheart and the apple of her father's eye—Robert even named his boat after her. My pregnancy had gone smoothly, although towards the end I had become more and more impatient with my increasing confinement to home.

Dr. John Macaulay, the longest-residing physician on Grand Manan, had stopped by at regular intervals to assure me that all was well or to pass the time of day on his way to and from other calls. He had arranged for Jeanette Laffoley, a practical nurse, to look after the housework and to assist him. At last it was time. Dr. Macaulay arrived and put me into a "twilight sleep" so I could remain conscious throughout the delivery without much discomfort or pain. Twenty-four hours later Maureen was born.

Dr. Macaulay had no office hours—he was available at any time, day or night, and he made house calls whenever necessary. Some of his patients were on White Head Island. To get there, he took the ferry that carried mail and passengers or hitched a ride on a fishing boat.

His first patient, in 1905, had been seven-year-old Gleason Green, not yet the boasting fisherman islanders loved so much. Dr. Macaulay drove by horse and buggy to the Green home in Ingalls Head. The boy had cut his arm with a knife, so the doctor plucked a hair from the tail of his horse and stitched the cut. He then went down the road to see Grove Ingalls. It was three in the morning. He delivered Mrs. Ingalls of twins, Lawrence and Luella, his first obstetrics case.

That long night set the pace for his entire practice. One other time, during a violent winter storm, he had a call from Mrs. Thomas Morgan of North Head. Dr. Macaulay left his Castalia home at midnight, walked along the shore, and reached her house at eight in the morning.

Dr. Macaulay carried a heavy load. There was no other physician on Grand Manan until World War II, let alone a hospital. He

When he was seven years old, in 1905, Gleason Green, the boasting fisherman adored by islanders, was Dr. John Macaulay's first patient. This picture was taken in the late twenties.

had to make his own decisions in nearly every case, and he did everything from tooth extraction to major surgery. Fortunately he had the help of his wife, Marion, as well as the assistance of several fine nurses who had been trained on mainland New Brunswick or in the United States: Maide Burnham of North Head and Beatrice Gaskill and Maude Dalzell, both of Castalia.

His practice was probably typical of all country doctors'. His office was located in his home, and I can still recall the sweet smell of chloroform that greeted me whenever I entered. Given the era, his nostrums, paregorics and laudanum, were typical, and the medical problems he faced were so often preventable—tuberculosis from drinking unpasteurized milk, consumption or lung cancer from heavy smoking.

Yet Dr. Macaulay was as dynamic and as daring as circumstances demanded. In 1937 a number of children contracted polio. One was Gleason Green's son, Pearley. Dr. Macaulay told Mrs. Green to massage the infected arm and shoulder and to exercise them. The treatment became known in 1942 as the Sister Kenny Method, after that woman had used it to combat paralysis from polio. It was effective. Pearley had many years of normal use of a badly infected arm.

Dr. Macaulay even treated Uncle Willie once in a while. Actually, my old friend was remarkably healthy. But one time he had a low-grade fever that persisted despite local ministrations, so the doctor shipped him to the hospital in St. Stephen for consultation. Nothing could keep the old man in bed for long, of course, and he was soon granted bathroom privileges. On his first trip to the privy he found himself without any toilet paper. He stuck his head out the door and cried to a nurse passing by, "Hey, Sister, there's no blasted paper in here."

"Well, you have a tongue, don't you?" the nurse chastised rather starchily.

"You're right, nurse," the old man chuckled. "But I ain't no damn cat."

In no time Uncle Willie was back home. He drove up to our place, old Sal trotting along as perky as ever.

"Well, you've been away, Uncle Willie," I called out from the front steps.

"Yep," he said, stepping down from the buggy and giving old Sal a nosebag of oats. "I been to that there Kleenex hospital in St. Stephen."

"And what did they discover?" I asked, almost afraid to hear the answer.

"Was nothin', Ina. They found water in my urine."

Soon after, the poor old man injured his thumb, and it became infected. Dr. Macaulay had to lance it and put in a few stitches. As he worked, he kept saying, "Now this won't hurt at all ... I'll sew it up ... You won't mind this one bit ..." Uncle Willie, more than a little nervous, squirmed at each touch.

Several months later the doctor was on Steamboat Wharf, waiting for the ferry to come in. As it arrived, islanders indulged in their usual entertainment, craning their necks to see who was disembarking, and enjoying the bizarre garb of the tourists. Uncle Willie was in the crowd, and he spotted Dr. Macaulay and went over to him. Never missing a trick, he soon noticed that the doctor's thumb was bandaged.

"Well, Doctor," Uncle Willie said, "I see you injured your thumb."

"Yes," Dr. Macaulay replied, "it became infected, and I had to lance it."

"Did it hurt?"

"Damn right it did!"

"That's strange," Uncle Willie noted. "When you lanced my thumb, you said it wouldn't hurt at all."

Like everyone else, though, Uncle Willie greatly appreciated the doctor's never-ending dedication. Dr. Macaulay and his wife rarely took a holiday—he wouldn't leave the island until he found a substitute, harder to get at that time—and he charged for his care, three dollars a house call, only when patients could afford it. But his devotion to duty, the prime rule of old-fashioned family doctors, finally caught up with him. In September 1939 he died of a heart attack, many names still outstanding on his books.

Dr. Macaulay was replaced by Dr. Russell Bryant, a young man just getting started. Also very much a "family" doctor, he did have regular office hours and a receptionist, to which folks soon became accustomed. In those days critically ill patients were whisked to hospital in Saint John or St. Stephen by the government-operated life-station boat, based on Outer Wood Island, off the shore at Seal Cove; from 1911 to 1934 the boat made fifty-three trips to St. Stephen. When I required emergency surgery in 1939, Dr. Bryant made me comfortable on our kitchen lounge and summoned the boat. The evacuation team arrived, lowered me onto the open deck, lashed the couch firmly and cleated it securely. Before I knew it, we were roaring across the Bay of Fundy at full throttle. All the while Dr. Bryant's firm hand squeezed my wrist reassuringly.

After a few years he moved to Sussex, New Brunswick, and was succeeded in turn by Dr. Railton Ritchie, Dr. Miroslav Spacek, and Dr. Jesus Dapena, who, by the way, married a Grand Manan girl. Dr. Spacek, for his part, loved to sail and spent much of his leisure time exploring the Grand Manan archipelago. He bought land on Outer Wood Island and raised sheep. He also bought the original Salvation Army hall in North Head, which he turned into a home for his retirement.

During the twenties and thirties the island had only one dentist, Dr. Carl Dexter. He maintained his practice in a small building at North Head, and he always gave effective local anaesthetics, for his work was relatively painless. He, too, married a Grand Manan girl, Mollie Gaskill, daughter of storeowners Joseph and Maude Gaskill, who had built the schooner *Kathleen and David.* After Dr. Dexter's death New Brunswick authorities couldn't find a replacement, so islanders had to take the ferry to the mainland. When there was only one trip a day, this meant staying overnight in a hotel, quite an expense for a simple filling or extraction. After World War II a mobile dental unit came from time to time to check the children's teeth.

～

By that time Maureen was a young woman. As a child, she was never any trouble. I stayed at home while she was growing up, except in 1934, when I filled in for a sick teacher. In 1942 I went back to work at Woodwards Cove because the trustees were not able to find anyone else. My salary was about seventy-five dollars a month, and we hired a housekeeper, Eliza Ingalls, who cared for us as if we were her own family.

Those were the hardest years of my teaching career, as Maureen was in my class. I taught her grades 7 and 8, and I always insisted that she behave as well as the other children—or better. She sure didn't like having to call me Mrs. Small. If there was a disruption in class, I invariably disciplined her too, because I didn't want the other children to think I was playing favourites.

But Maureen was a stellar student who applied herself to her lessons and tolerated my repeated drilling at home. As far as I was concerned, our daughter was going to have the best education possible, and that included attending a good high school. Although the schools at North Head and Grand Harbour offered upper grades by the early thirties, most children usually left school after Grade 8, lured by the appeal of the sea.

Discussions concerning the construction of a high school had begun as far back as 1927. At a meeting of the Grand Manan Parent–Teacher's Association in 1943, the issue came to the fore, and it was decided that two teachers should visit Deer Island, which had built, and was running, a successful high school. A North Head teacher, Mina Cook, and I were chosen to go and

Robert named his boat after our daughter. The Maureen Nelda *is docked in front of the Robert M. Small Factory.*

gather information on the cost, planning, and execution of such a project. At the time, I was also on the Woodwards Cove board of trustees.

At Deer Island, north of Campobello, we were greeted by a Mr. Welch, the chairman of the school board. He drove us to the high school, where we received a wealth of information and practical advice from administrators and teachers. They showed us the actual plans for the project, pointed out what was good and bad about the final product, and outlined the costs in detail. They assured us that a high school on Grand Manan would not raise taxes all that much. Mina and I arrived home that evening, our heads full of plans and ideas.

For the next meeting of the PTA we prepared an estimate of costs. Then I attended open PTA meetings in each village in an attempt to sell the plan to islanders. In some villages my pleas fell on deaf ears. At Castalia, in particular, the meeting was stormy because people feared their taxes would sky rocket. A vocal delegation, many of whom, by the way, did not have school-age children, rejected any notion of a high school. Voices shouted, "Stay home, Ina. We don't want your crazy ideas ... Mind your own damn business, lady ... Go home, Ina Small, you're nothing but a stranger from away ..." I wanted to reply in kind, but for once I bit my tongue and refused to enter into a slinging match. I knew I was fighting for a good cause.

I had help. Elmer Wilcox, the electrician–plumber who had fixed our kitchen pump, gave unstinting devotion to the project. He had learned his trade in Boston and had returned home to support all worthwhile causes—the high school, the hospital, the museum, the senior citizen's home. If he received a call concerning any public building, he dropped whatever he was doing and came to the rescue.

Numerous others lobbied long and hard for the high school, and finally the issue came to a vote at school-board meetings in each district. All but two, Castalia and North Head, voted in favour. The project was delayed again, for another year. Even those who had supported the high school felt that paved roads should come first—in spring and sometimes in fall the roads turned into seas of mud, often becoming impassable. Nonetheless, those who had voted *yes* went to work on the die-hard opposition. The argument they used was simple but effective: the children of Grand Manan deserved a better education than their parents or grandparents had obtained. It didn't take long to convince North Head residents, who had voted *no* because they wanted the school located in their village, not in Grand Harbour. Castalia citizens were a different matter. In the spring of 1944 Dr. W.K. Tibert, head of vocational schools for New Brunswick, and Dr. Amos Anderson, superintendent of schools for Charlotte County, attended a special meeting at Castalia. This session was stormier than all the others put together. It was a close call, but when the final tally was taken, the verdict was clear. There would be a high school.

I had the privilege of choosing the members of the first board of trustees, the only time the board members weren't elected. To be fair, I selected one representative from each village (only one is still living, Gleason Green); for chairman, I chose Fletcher Harvey of Seal Cove. He had not been enthusiastic in the beginning, but everyone knew that once the high school was set to go, he would give it untiring support.

The high school opened at Grand Harbour in the fall of 1948, soon after work had begun on a "million-dollar highway." Howard Douglas was the principal, and Charles Titus was the custodian. Thirteen students graduated that first year, some going on to college and trade school, and as time went by, many students received the prized Beaverbrook scholarships, as well as other awards. With students from all over the island travelling to Grand Harbour, construction began on a new high school in the late 1960s. In 1977 the old high school became an elementary school, and the little one-, two-, and three-room schoolhouses were closed forever.

In 1944 Maureen completed Grade 8. I knew that the high school would come to fruition but not in time to include our daughter as a student. I told Robert that she *must* have a proper secondary education.

"Ina," he said, "Maureen only needs Grade 8. We both know she will be comfortable, thanks to the factory. She can settle down here, marry, and live quite happily. She'll want for nothing."

A vision of Maureen working in the fish factory flashed before my eyes. In an instant my mind was made up. "I'm leaving, Robert."

"Please, Ina ..."

"No, I'm taking Maureen to the mainland. I shall obtain work there and see that she goes to high school in the fall. And that's that." I looked Robert straight in the eye, but he did not reply.

Within a fortnight Robert was driving us to the ferry. He was silent until we were ready to board. "If you need anything, Ina, anything at all, phone me."

I couldn't speak. Maureen was in tears as she clung to her father. Resolutely I bade the island a silent farewell, and Maureen and I walked onto the ferry. I went into the passenger's lounge, and Maureen stayed on deck, waving at the receding jetty and the lone figure of her father until the steamer swung past Swallowtail Light and he was no longer in sight. The ferry set course for Saint John and steamed steadily ahead to our new future.

Politics and Patriotism

Oh, loyal Tory supporters
There are facts that you must know
The Liberals get quite ruthless
When putting on their show
They enumerate each tombstone
Each stranger from away
And a certain party member
Votes twice election day

When it served their purposes, Grand Mananers stood up for their rights. But their flawless island instinct told most locals that there was always something fishy about politics.

The mating dance of provincial politicians with the people was a familiar one. Each party put on a supper, and if you sat down to eat, you were obliged to stay and listen to the speeches of that party's candidates. Canny islanders, however, did not always observe political protocol—many of them ducked out after gulping down a second piece of pie.

At one particular election supper in the 1930s, I felt well fed by the Liberal constituency association, so I settled down for the long haul. No doubt prompted by a rapidly diminishing audience, party officials wound the evening up surprisingly fast. The keynote speaker was a prominent Deer Island Liberal, Foster Calder, a far better speaker than the local candidate. On my way out I shook hands with him, and he rewarded me with a political story for the record.

"It was at the conclusion of an evening such as this, Ina," he began. "I was shaking hands with a number of people and urging each of them to vote for the Liberal slate. An elderly woman, the kind you would call a dear old lady, came up to me and thanked me profusely for my address. 'I just love to hear you speak, you have such a ... such a mellow voice.' She shook my hand and moved out the door.

" 'That's strange,' muttered my campaign manager, 'I always thought she was a Conservative.' Well, to make a long story short, Ina, when I got home, I decided to look up the word *mellow* in the dictionary. I read: '*mellow* ... juicy with ripeness, softened by age ... rotten.' As usual my manager was right. That 'dear old lady' was certainly no Liberal!"

Neither was I for that matter. Before I left for the mainland in 1944, Robert and I were in agreement on most issues, but politics was *not* one of them. He was a Liberal as was his father before him. I argued with Robert, but it was no use. "Look, Robert," I said, "if your father was a fool, that's no reason you should be one!" Robert smiled at me and voted Liberal. I smiled in the polling booth and negated his vote.

The McLean brothers of Blacks Harbour, on the mainland, were staunch Liberal politicians in the years before World War II. They owned the largest sardine factory in the British Empire, and they had a good deal of influence on the island. But not quite enough. Grand Manan voted in a long-time Conservative to the legislature. Scott Guptill, instrumental in getting the fishermen's marketing board started during the Depression, served nearly twenty-five years in office. Gale McLaughlin, a Conservative, succeeded him. Then Leon Small won the seat. Leon, in turn, was succeeded by the popular Eric Allaby, teacher, museum curator, historian and, incidentally, Liberal.

The important thing on election day was to get out and vote. Each candidate sent out representatives to make sure every single supporter turned up at the polls. Not all islanders exercised their franchise willingly, or should I say knowingly.

In one Depression-era provincial contest the day of decision dawned. A Liberal-party worker turned up at the door of a set of identical twins at Castalia, to drive them to the polls. The only way anybody could tell these twins apart was that one had a full beard and the other was clean shaven. Alas, the clean-shaven twin was ill in bed. So the driver took the bearded twin to the voting station at the public hall in Castalia. After he voted, the worker took him to the barber and treated him to a shave and a haircut. Then it was back to the polls to cast the vote of his sick brother.

The sick twin really was not well at all. In a few days his brother called Dr. Macaulay. By now the patient was ranting away in a feverish delerium.

"What's wrong with my brother?" asked the well twin.

"I'm not sure I know," the doctor said after deliberating for several moments. "Tell me, does he act this way when he's alone?"

"I don't rightly know, Doctor. I never was with him when he was alone."

~

Though island politics may have been tainted with scepticism, wartime brought out everyone's deep-seated attachment to King and Country. A tradition of service had been established during World War I, and it resurfaced during World War II. The island Red Cross went into full swing, with many of us volunteering our services to knit and sew, including Grace Ingersoll and Carrie Daggett, both of Seal Cove, and Maide Burnham. Alice Draper helped out, too. She was still looking after the Woodwards Cove post office—and still arguing with her husband. Actually, it was Pete who suggested she get involved, but he thought she should donate blood. According to him, her "fightin' blood" would help win the war in no time.

Roberta Ingalls of Grand Harbour was secretary of the local Red Cross, and I was work convenor. My job required ordering yarn from Saint John, distributing it throughout the island, and fetching the finished articles. We knitted Balaclava helmets, socks, scarves, mitts, and sleeveless pullovers. All the Red Cross members met at North Head, in a room above Joseph Gaskill's store, and inspected each article of clothing carefully to make sure it was knitted according to specifications (few items needed correcting). Then we packed the items and readied the parcels for shipping overseas.

After the war many Grand Manan women received service pins from the Red Cross. Roberta Ingalls and I received our quarter-century pins in 1965. Mine is one of my most treasured possessions.

～

It was during the war years that everyone realized the need for an island hospital. The greatest obstacle was acquiring a building, for the Canadian government needed every penny for the war effort.

Then fate intervened. Frank Ingersoll, Sr., had a new home at North Head—Sabra Jane had bought the old one—but he and his wife spent their winters in St. Stephen. One day, just after the war started, they went out for a drive. Not far from St. Stephen, their car stalled on the tracks at a railway crossing. An oncoming train was unable to stop in time, and they were both killed instantly.

Frank and his wife had bequeathed their North Head home as an island hospital. Now that the structure was no longer a problem, the Red Cross women worked hard to raise money for renovations and additions—an elevator, nurses' accommodations, equipment, and furniture. In 1940 we held a fall hospital fair at Grand Harbour. We sold hot dogs and hamburgers and arts and crafts; we had games and rides, including a merry-go-round. The week-long fair raised more than a thousand dollars.

Then Mary McMurtry of North Head, wife of the skipper of the ferry, canvassed mainland firms for donations. Finally we published a Grand Manan cookbook. We asked all good island cooks to send in their favourite recipes, and they soon poured in from every village.

Delia Ingalls's Devilled Scallops

1 lb. scallops, 1 clove garlic, chopped, 2 tbsps. melted butter, flour, 1/2 tsp. dry mustard, 2 tsps. horse radish, 1/2 tsp. celery salt, 2 tbsps. chopped parsley, 1 tbsp. lemon juice, 1/8 tsp. pepper, 2 tbsps. butter, melted, 1/2 cup soft bread crumbs.

Cut scallops in quarters. Cook garlic in melted butter until tender; blend in flour; add mustard, horse radish, celery salt, parsley, lemon juice and pepper. Mix thoroughly and add scallops. Cook four to five minutes, stirring constantly. Place in four well greased individual casseroles or six ounce custard cups. Combine two tbsps. melted butter and bread crumbs; sprinkle over top of each dish. Bake in 350°F. oven 15 to 20 minutes or until brown.

Sabra Jane Briggs's Ginger Ale Salad

Soak 2 tbsps. gelatin in 4 tbsps. cold water. Dissolve it in 1/2 cup boiling fruit juice. Add: 1/2 cup sugar, 1/8 tsp. salt, 1 pint ginger ale, juice of 1 lemon. Chill these ingredients until the jelly is nearly set. Then combine it with the following: 1/2 lb. grapes, seeded, 1 orange, skinned and sliced, 6 slices canned pineapple, cut in cubes, 1/4 lb. candied ginger, chopped. Place the salad in a wet mold. Chill it and unmold it on lettuce. Serve it with cream mayonnaise.

Roberta Ingalls's Peanut Butter Cake

4 tbsps. shortening, 1/2 cup peanut butter, 1 1/4 cups white sugar, 3 eggs, 1 cup milk, 2 1/4 cups flour, 4 tsps. baking powder, 1 tsp. salt.

Method: Cream shortening, peanut butter and sugar. Add beaten eggs. Blend well. Bake in layers.

Filling: 4 tbsps. peanut butter, 2 tbsps. butter. Ice with chocolate butter icing to which a small portion of peanut butter has been added.

Ina Small's Pecan Balls

1 cup butter, 1/4 cup white sugar, 2 cups flour (don't sift), salt, 2 tsps. vanilla, 1/2 cup nuts (can use walnuts).

Mix and roll in one inch diameter balls, cook in 350° oven about 15 minutes. While still warm, roll in icing sugar.

The Grand Manan Cook Book *sold so well because it contained some delicious island fare.*

Sabra Jane and I collected them. I sorted them into sections and typed many of them, as did Marie Thomas, secretary of the school board. Once again mainland firms helped out, by buying advertisements.

The revenue from the advertising paid for the printing costs, and we ran off five thousand copies of the cookbook, selling them instantly at a dollar apiece. Two more reprintings of one thousand copies each followed in quick succession, and they were sold in various stores. The drugstore at North Head and the Cheney store at Grand Harbour constantly reordered copies to supply the insatiable demand. With those first three printings, the Red Cross raised seven thousand dollars for the hospital, no small sum in 1940. Believe it or not, the cookbook is still in print, raising money for many worthwhile island endeavours.

The Red Cross Outpost Hospital opened in 1941 with fourteen beds and a nursery. Clearly too small for the island population, it was torn down and replaced with a concrete structure in 1971.

Uncle Willie was one of the first patients in the old hospital. In 1941 he suffered a bout of pneumonia that set him back a few weeks. By then my old friend was the grand age of ninety, but he was still as spry and as witty as ever, though his constant companion, old Sal, was long gone.

In hospital Uncle Willie met his match. There was another old-timer in one of the beds next to him, and he was blind in one eye. "I can see more with one eye than you can with two," the old-timer said to Uncle Willie.

"Oh, no you can't."

"Yes I can. You can see only my one eye, and I can see your two."

A little later Uncle Willie rang the bell for the nurse. When she arrived, he said, "Nurse, I want to shit." Horrified, the nurse told him that that was not a nice way to talk and that he should say "number two."

Uncle Willie nodded obligingly, but in a few minutes he rang the bell again. The nurse came and asked Uncle Willie what he wanted this time. "That boy in the next bed, nurse, he said he wants to shit, too, but you never gave him a number."

When I visited my old friend in hospital, he was quick to testify to the efficiency of the medical staff. Having no pyjamas, Uncle Willie kept on his underwear. A few days before, the doctor had come in to make his examination. It must have been fast, for poor Uncle Willie complained in a choking voice, "Why, he ripped those underpants off quicker than you could skin a codfish."

Hospital visits resulted in some strange confidences being exchanged with local ministers. The Reverend Mr. Edsforth, an

The Red Cross Outpost Hospital opened in 1941 with fourteen beds and a nursery.

Anglican priest, was making the rounds in the hospital when he spotted an old friend, Sam Greenlaw, an odd-job man from North Head. Sam had something that he needed to get off his chest in a hurry. "Now, what do you suppose Virginia has done while I'm here?"

"I wouldn't know," answered the reverend.

"She has put in a toilet ... a flush."

"Well now, I'm sure you'll all find it useful."

"Maybe so," said Sam. "But the next time I'm in hospital, I wouldn't be surprised if she put in a bathtub. Now, what in the world would we want a bathtub for?"

⌒

During World War II everyone kept their eyes peeled. From time to time fishermen spotted submarines off the coast, but we all wondered about the enemy within. Were there foreign agents at work on our small island?

Grand Manan occupies a key position in the Bay of Fundy. If a hostile force had ever taken possession of the island, it would have been in a strategic position to obstruct coastal shipping, as well as to overthrow New England, Nova Scotia, and New Brunswick.

Grand Manan took no chances. Early in the war a volunteer reserve army corps was established, with headquarters at the

Masonic Hall in Woodwards Cove. Trained by officers of the regular army, this force kept round-the-clock lookouts at the northern and southern ends of the island and at other strategic locations. All islanders were asked to report any unusual activities, any submarine sightings, any strangers.

I remember one strange woman from away. She was a tall brunette with a voluptuous figure, and she wore heavy-framed horn-rimmed glasses that obscured her face. She settled at Woodwards Cove in early 1940 and stayed for nearly a year. Although she claimed she was a writer, she never produced anything, except for an unusual chart. This woman visited every nook and cranny of the island, and soon she knew it better than the locals. She took photographs of anything and everything, and she drew a map that included every imaginable detail—buoys, lighthouses, wharves, breakwaters, channels. Her landlady caught a glimpse of the final diagram, and she was amazed at the accuracy of the information gleaned by her mysterious lodger.

On a regular basis, the tall brunette sent off fat, bulging letters to an address in South America, but she never received any mail at all—highly unusual, we all thought, especially in wartime. She might have been writing those long letters to a sweetheart in the forces, but given the South American address, we wondered *whose* forces. Then one day, without a word to anyone, the woman hopped the steamer and disappeared. No one has ever seen or heard from her since.

Much later in the war another woman appeared. In many ways she fit the profile of the earlier mystery woman. Word soon arrived that a patrol boat with two intelligence officers was on its way from the mainland to question her. Perhaps forewarned, she flew the coop; that is, she and a gentleman friend rowed to the United States on the very same day her inquisitors were due to arrive. Of course, it could have been a romantic adventure, a somewhat athletic wartime elopement.

There's no doubt that war does strange things to people, makes them think strange thoughts. One afternoon, Grand Harbour fisherman Edgar Cook woke up from a nap with a start. "Something has happened to my George!" he cried. That night he received a telegram announcing the death of his son. George Cook was the first Grand Manan casualty of World War II.

Many other men and boys died in the conflict. The War Memorial by the Anglican Church of the Ascension in North Head bears the names of those fatalities. Each year, on November 11, a memorial service is held lest we forget.

Progress

On the Grand Manan ferry
You're sure of a very tempestuous ride
If your poor belly shakes like a jelly
Just lean over the side!

"No, I'm taking Maureen to the mainland. I shall obtain work there and see that she goes to high school in the fall. And that's that."

With those words, I had ripped apart my sixteen-year marriage and left Grand Manan. Maureen was thirteen when we took up residence in Saint John. For a year I taught at La Tour School, while taking an evening commercial course at the Modern Business College. Then I taught business administration at Saint John Vocational School. Maureen, meanwhile, went to a proper high school. Sometimes Robert came to visit us, sometimes Maureen went to see him. I did not accompany her.

When Maureen graduated, my sole purpose for being on the mainland had been served. I missed the island, but most of all I missed Robert, his deep brown eyes, his patience, his companionship. Here was a man with absolutely no pretensions, a man untainted by innate snobbishness. How I must have stung him. Maureen was now a young woman attending normal school, and I knew I must pocket my foolish stubborn pride, beg Robert's forgiveness, and return to Grand Manan.

It was a cold, foggy morning in 1948 when Robert met me at the ferry. We said very little to each other. I held out my hand, and he squeezed it with both of his. We drove down the island to Woodwards Cove. At last I was home. So many things had changed. Sadly, there were gaps in the ranks of my friends. Dear Uncle Willie had passed away quietly in his sleep one night at the age of ninety-six. I could almost hear him chuckling, "Time to go, Ina, time to go." Alice Draper was dead, too, and Pete had sold the store and moved to the mainland.

Progress with a capital *P* had come to Grand Manan. The high school was open, and the little hospital was proving its worth. The fishing boats were bigger and better, equipped with ship-to-shore radios. The main road was paved, and lo and behold, there was an airstrip at North Head.

Robert's cousin Oscar Small had opened the flying field in 1947. He was always in the tiny waiting room when a plane arrived. His wife, Lula, kept a record of all the flights from Saint John, answered calls concerning arrivals and departures, and generally helped keep things going smoothly. Their son Basil now owns the airport. (The original airport is no longer operating. The summer of 1988 saw the opening of a new one farther inland, away from fogs and cliffs.)

One 1948 flight brought in a mechanic from Eastport to repair the engine of Ralph Green's fishing boat. Ralph was the son-in-law of Jeanette Laffoley, the practical nurse who had assisted me during my pregnancy. Then Gordon Brooks of White Head Island was flown to St. Stephen for medical attention after an accident on his boat.

The first helicopter mercy mission to the island was a dramatic event. Mrs. Medric LeBlanc had taken seriously ill. A naval helicopter was dispatched from the Shearwater base in Halifax to evacuate Mrs. LeBlanc to the mainland. But by that time it was dark, and the landing strip had no lights. As Lula Small reported in the *Quoddy Tides* (Eastport), Oscar rallied together North Head residents: "Neighbours circled the runway with their cars, and by the light of their headlamps, the helicopter was able to arrive safely." The winds were favourable, so the helicopter quickly took off with the sick woman. An ambulance stood by at the Saint John airport and rushed her to hospital. Mrs. Leblanc's recovery was successful.

Vernon Stuart, a retired fisherman from Deer Island, obtained his pilot's licence and flew forty free mercy flights from Grand Manan in five years. On one occasion he rushed a special type of blood plasma from Saint John to Grand Manan for an emergency case at the island hospital. Vernon flew his own Piper Cub, and his permanent base was Oscar's airport. He became known as The Flying Fisherman.

~

By the end of 1948 businessmen were taking advantage of the quick way to Grand Manan, using the Saint John flying service. It was no wonder they chose to fly: the ferry service hadn't improved at all. In fact, it had become worse.

The first regular ferry to the island was launched in 1884 by the Grand Manan Steamship Company. Named the *Flushing,* she provided four trips a week to the mainland. Captain John Ingersoll was in charge of the old steamer. She left at exactly seven in the morning, and Captain Ingersoll himself had to walk from Seal Cove to North Head, a good fifteen miles. In winter he carried a shovel to dig his way through the drifting snow. He always made

With Maureen's graduation from high school, my sole purpose for staying on the mainland had been served.

it—North Head folks set their watches by the departure of the *Flushing.*

In 1900 she was replaced by the steamer *Aurora,* renamed the *Grand Manan* in 1911. She served the island until 1930, when the *Grand Manan II* was pressed into service by a mainland concern, Eastern Canada Coastal Steamships Ltd., which had bought out the Grand Manan company in 1929. The *Grand Manan II* was diesel powered, and, what's more, it was a roll-on ferry with a capacity for twelve cars.

But you can't have cream forever. The *Grand Manan II* was sold to the West Indies at the start of the war and was succeeded by the *Keith Cann,* which had little or no capacity for vehicles. The *Keith Cann,* in turn, was replaced in 1944 by the *Grand Manan III.* At its best it had room for nine cars.

As in the old days, the days before 1930, cargo, freight, and cars were loaded onto the ferry by derrick and winch. Passengers drove slowly along the jetty until they were near the stern of the boat. Then seamen attached hoisting gear to the vehicle. If a passenger was brave enough, he watched as his car, swinging wildly, was lifted into the air by a single line. A seaman on deck lowered the vehicle to a spot as close as possible to the next car.

When people finally boarded the ferry themselves, they could sit in their cars on deck and enjoy a breath of fresh sea air. This prevented many passengers from becoming sick as the boat pitched and rolled and yawed across the bay. They also had a fine view until their vehicles received a thick covering of salty spray. As soon as their cars were unloaded on the mainland, owners had them washed immediately, before the salt ate away the paint.

At that time, there were five trips a week, mostly to Saint John. The schedules were somewhat complex, too. Here is one example:

Monday: North Head-Campobello-Eastport-St. Andrews-North Head
Tuesday: North Head-Saint John
Wednesday: Saint John-North Head
Thursday: North Head-St. Andrews-St. Stephen-North Head
Friday: North Head-Saint John-North Head

All Grand Mananers had a rough time with the rules and regulations on the ferry. A few years before his death Uncle Willie ventured to the mainland. He bought his ticket and was headed for a seat aft when a deck officer called out to him: "Sir, your ticket!" Uncle Willie came back and watched in dismay as the official punched several holes in it. "Here you are, sir, thank you," said the officer, handing back the ticket.

The introduction of the Grand Manan III *marked a step backwards in island transportation.*

Uncle Willie was not at all pleased. "What did you go and do that fer?" he asked in frustration. "That was a fresh ticket. I jist bought it. I don't want no damn ticket full of holes. You keep it. I'll get a new one." With some difficulty, the deck officer persuaded the old man to hang on to it, assuring him that it was perfectly valid for the return voyage.

On his return Uncle Willie was approached by a tourist. I guess he looked as though he would know a great deal about the island.

"I suppose you have lived all your days on Grand Manan, sir," the tourist said.

"Nope," replied the old man. "Not yet."

There were some old-timers on Grand Manan who never once left the island, let alone took the ferry. They didn't have radio, either, so their knowledge of the outside world was scanty. Belinda, a neighbour of Uncle Willie's, was like that. She chewed tobacco, smoked an old pipe, and lived to be almost a hundred. Nothing ever seemed to bother her.

In spring or fall the *Grand Manan III* was taken off for a paint job or refit. She could be in drydock for two or three weeks at a time. Then tugs or fishing boats were pressed into service. The replacement vessels carried about twelve passengers. The captains of those small boats had real problems because many times more than a dozen turned up. Being Grand Mananers, the skippers hated to turn anyone away, especially students on the Saint John side who were trying to get home for holidays.

One Easter, Captain George Merriam, a mainlander, was faced with that old problem. When he docked at Saint John, a large number of young people were on the jetty. He decided to risk it. Cautioning each person that he travelled at his own risk, he jammed every one of the waiting mob aboard his boat. It was standing room only, but the passengers couldn't have cared less. The vessel made safe passage, and later that day families from one end of the island to the other enjoyed happy reunions. But one blabbermouth spoiled everything by telling the Maritime authorities. The hero of that Easter weekend was fined for his kindness.

Eventually, Grand Mananers became fed up. They united, and hollered loud and long for an improved ferry service. They blockaded Fisherman's Wharf, where the ferry now docked, for nearly a week. Finally, the authorities listened. In 1965 the new *Grand Manan* came into service. Things improved almost overnight. She carried up to twenty-nine cars, and there was no more derrick and winch. It took about an hour and a half to sail from North Head to Blacks Harbour.

There was one drawback, however: the improvement in service brought an increase in traffic. To catch the early-morning ferry, people had to line up the previous afternoon. This heralded the beginning of a unique island endeavour. Enterprising islanders bought old trucks, and for a mere five dollars they parked them in the ferry line-up to save places for travellers. With twenty sailings a week in peak season, these entrepreneurs were bringing in one hundred dollars every seven days. They currently charge ten dollars, but their booming business may slow down, as people can now buy tickets a day in advance.

~

Before 1965 the poor ferry service did not deter Grand Mananers from travelling frequently to the mainland or to Maine. Islanders were in the habit of shopping on the American side, and they had to declare anything they bought. A large customs office was located at the corner of the road turning off to Fisherman's Wharf, and a uniformed customs officer met the ferry when it docked.

Of course, Grand Mananers seemed to suffer notoriously bad memories on all such official occasions. I'm not suggesting for a moment that they were out and out criminals. Rather they were enterprising seafaring stock who recognized a favourable breeze when it blew up and steered their course accordingly. So it was that on more than one occasion, an islander might feel a little chilly and slip into an extra sweater or two, purchased in Eastport, before undertaking the cold voyage home. I myself recall wearing a completely new outfit—dress, warm coat, and hat—on such a homecoming. With tongue in cheek, the customs officer remarked, "Good afternoon, Mrs. Small. My, don't we look especially natty today."

Fresh fruit was also a great temptation for islanders. Sometimes, especially during the winter months, they bought American strawberries. But they had to smuggle them past the cold eyes of the "revenooer." They couldn't even pay duty on those strawberries, as they were forbidden fruit. The customs officer quickly confiscated them and then just as quickly dumped them into the ocean.

Some villages on Grand Manan had their own customs officer as well. There was so much interisland fishing traffic that it was expedient to clear customs locally. With the exception of the officers at Seal Cove and North Head, the customs officers worked out of their own homes. Small boats were rarely searched unless there was reason to believe they were carrying contraband. On the American side boats needed papers to land. There was a small charge for this—fifty cents—clearance I think they called it. This fee increased as did everything else.

The customs officer in Woodwards Cove was Perry (P.M.) Small, Connie Lambert's uncle and our neighbour. More often than not, P.M. found a pail of lard or a couple of tins of American coffee on his doorstep. Simple thank yous, I guess. In any event, P.M. never told.

One reason Grand Mananers shopped so much in the United States, and on the mainland, was that goods were cheaper. Freight and handling costs, especially when cargo was loaded and unloaded by derrick, sometimes added as much as 25 percent to mainland prices. As islanders used to say, "The steamboat makes the rules!"

Post-war inflation sent food prices up beyond belief. Some cuts of beef were getting close to a dollar a pound. Butter had soared to sixty cents a pound; bread, thirty-three cents a loaf; and tea, fifty cents a pound. Local storekeepers had no choice but to charge according to increasing freight and wholesale costs.

Wally Lambert of Castalia sold fresh meat in his store, a rarity after the war. One regular customer thought that the Sunday roast was a bit too expensive. "Wally," he remarked, "I've always wanted a brand new car. Thanks to you, I know how to get one."

"How?" Wally asked.

"I've got this old critter down home. Now if I kill her and peddle horse meat at half your prices, I'll surely have more than enough to get me a new Olds."

~

Despite rising prices and improved equipment such as refrigerators, the small stores never changed in one way. They were still peopled by characters swapping stories and telling jokes, reminding me of the early days at the Drapers' place.

Roy Ingalls ran a store at Grand Harbour, later operated by his son Austin. One day old Roy told a customer named Wilcox, "My neighbour jist died. Must have left a lot of money."

The customer could not resist the opportunity to let fly with a familiar chestnut: "Well, Roy, I figger he couldn't take it with him."

Sir Charles and Lady Ames were regular summer visitors. Sir Charles was a stockbroker, and Lady Ames had a rather high opinion of herself. She thought that locals should give her special attention, something unheard of on Grand Manan.

One day she was shopping at the Newton Brothers Store in Grand Harbour. Nelson Hettrick was the butcher. Lady Ames had bought some meat but returned for another cut. She thought that Nelson should leave the customer he was serving and tend to her. "Young man," she said, "my name is Lady Ames, and I would like to be waited on."

"Yes, ma'am," Nelson said, "and *I'm* Lord Nelson. How do you do?" Incidentally, both Sir Charles and Lady Ames are buried in the Anglican cemetery at North Head. Neither of them has been in a hurry lately.

Si Cheney kept the post office at Grand Harbour. One time he hired John Wilson to put a new foundation under his house. After John had been working for a few hours, Si came to the cellar door and called down, "John, have you seen any cats yet?"

"No, no, Mr. Cheney, I haven't seen any cats yet."

Si came back in a while and asked the same question and received the same answer. This happened three times. Young John was consumed by curiosity. "Why do you keep asking about cats, Mr. Cheney?"

"Well, it's this way, John. I've seen thousands of cats go under there, but none come out."

Si was a character behind the wicket. He looked up one day and saw a regular come into the post office with his dog. The animal was fond of Si, so he rushed to the wicket and, tail wagging, put his paws up on the counter. Si peered over his glasses and said, "Hell, dog, there's no mail for you."

Tales of Two Islands

The bell in the steeple has not been rung
Not a member has come to sit in a pew
No sermon was preached, not a hymn was sung
Like a ship on the sea, without any crew....
—Archer Coy Wilcox

"Come on, Ina, the lunch is all packed. Let's go!" It was the summer of 1959, and my friends were taking me to Two Islands for a picnic. We got in their fancy motor boat at Seal Cove and drove a few miles southeast. The sea was quiet, so we made fast passage. We tied the boat to the wharf, badly in need of repair, and followed the shore road to the old settlement.

The legendary Captain Kidd is said to have taken refuge in these parts. Chased by a British man-of-war, the pirate, according to legend, sailed his ship into Two Islands Harbour. Some say his band of pirates spent the winter there. One man may even have jumped ship. Perhaps he was the first Wilcox to come to these parts. Who knows? Such a tale only adds spice to the romantic past.

The trail was grown over with grass and weeds, but I could still see the wheel tracks of wagons that had travelled the road so many years ago. Only horses and mules had hauled supplies then, and I could almost hear the snorting and the creaking of the old carts as we walked along.

We looked at the old houses—some small, others large—with decorative wooden mouldings around the eaves. Every once in a while the tall grass revealed remnants of a garden. Lilac bushes and other untrimmed shrubs were growing wild. There were the remains of an ancient car rusting beside a house. Some enterprising resident had brought it there by scow and then abandoned it.

The road curved and went up a knoll. On either side were lovely roses, "June roses" we used to call them. They seemed to beckon us to the little church that lay ahead. The small frame building looked as though it had been recently painted. Its steeple stood proud and tall, and not a single sparkling window was broken. The tiny cemetery opposite the church was enclosed by a neat fence. In front were hitching posts, where some early churchgoers had tethered their horses. Solid concrete steps led into the vestibule. Who had built cement steps long before the churches on Grand Manan had such fine construction? The church had been built in

1918, with gas lamps to brighten the interior. Then, in the proud tradition of Two Islands, the congregation had installed a gasoline-driven generating plant, becoming the first to have its place of worship lit by electricity. How devoted and dedicated those pioneers must have been—money was never plentiful in those days.

The abandoned church was in excellent condition. The door was locked, but as I peeked through a window, the bright sunshine gave a warm look to the interior. It was as if this little church was just waiting to welcome its congregation. The Bible was open on the pulpit, the hymn books lay on the organ. In my mind I saw the minister standing at the front of the church, the choir in its place, the congregation ready to join in worship. Did I know any of those faces? Oh yes, yes I did.

How well I remembered Two Islands. The larger one was Inner Wood Island, the smaller was Outer Wood. It's possible that centuries ago Witch's Point joined the northern tip of Inner Wood to Red Point, on the mainland of Grand Manan. As well, Ross, Cheney, and White Head islands could have been joined, and Long Point could have been connected to Gannet Rock. The Cross Jacks (part of the Murr Ledges), Southern Long Ledge, Western Ledge, Wallace Rocks, Southeast Breaker, and Seal Cove all could have been headlands of the area. Seal Cove Sound may well have been a small lake once upon a time, for the water at Belle Buoy is shallow, only twenty-eight feet deep.

Erosion, that irresistible force of the winds and the wild sea, had relentlessly changed the shape of the land. But I was concerned with another kind of erosion—the wearing away of small communities, the end of an era of pioneer settlement, the erosion of a way of life.

After the turn of the century, there was a bustling settlement of about one hundred souls on Inner Wood Island. Before that old church was built, regular Sunday service had been held in the schoolhouse, with the minister at Seal Cove coming over to lead sermons. If there was a morning service at Seal Cove, the service on Inner Wood was held in the evening. If passage was impossible or if the minister was detained, one of the elders of the church, Abel or Eugene Wilcox, conducted worship. Otherwise, Chester Green rowed out to a large boat and brought the parson over.

Chester also carried the mail from Grand Manan, often assisted by his brother-in-law Percy Green. In summer they rode bicycles up from the wharf, but in winter they slung the heavy sacks over

There was a lot of traffic between Seal Cove Harbour and Two Islands.

their backs and walked up to the tiny post office. The winter mail included heavy parcels, as well as the regular bundles of letters.

The post office also contained a store, selling candy and delicious homemade ice cream. Inner Wood Island was the first place that you could buy ice cream. On warm Saturday nights it was a great adventure to row over to Two Islands, gorge on ice cream, and really make a night of it.

It wasn't until the twenties that Grand Manan had ice-cream parlours, one called Verona's in Grand Harbour and the other at Oscar Locke's place in North Head. (During World War II, the Red Cross built a small stand on Inner Wood and staffed it with a number of volunteers who made and sold ice cream. There were four delicious flavours to tempt visitors from Grand Manan: banana, vanilla, pineapple, and chocolate. That old building is now falling down.)

Inner Wood Island even had three telephones, connected to Grand Manan by underwater cable. Because there was a life-saving station at Shag Head, at the tip of Outer Wood, the provincial government had supplied the phones free of charge. From the post office, people could phone the station when boats were lost or in trouble. The station had been built in 1911, with about a dozen men working shifts. Every night the man in charge lit a lantern, attached it to a pole, and hoisted it as high as it would go. At different times George Maker, James Daggett, Albert Ripley, Andy Nelson (later drowned), and Mabury Russell all served at Shag Head. Coleman Green was one of the last to do duty; Wellington Flagg, whose children gave their names to the schooner *Kathleen and David*, served at the station until it was abandoned in the forties.

One of the earliest pioneers on Grand Manan was Charles Dyer Wilcox, builder of the *Exile*. He settled at Deep Cove in 1816 to ply his trade. One night, between sundown and dark, he saw a casket. He told his wife about the vision and remarked that he wasn't going to live much longer. Inside of a week, at fifty-seven, he was dead.

His descendants moved to Two Islands to be nearer to the outer fishing grounds. Charles's grandson, Leaman Wilcox, lived at the western end of Outer Wood Island, as did his brothers, Alfred and Abel. They were among the original settlers on Outer Wood. Abel, however, eventually moved to Inner Wood, owning the post office. All three were successful fishermen.

Abel Wilcox might well have been called Able. He could line up eleven molasses barrels and then jump in and out of each in turn, hardly drawing a breath. No mean feat. He was also a wonderful character. One of his neighbours, Andrew Cheney, dropped in to visit Abel one day. Recalling early Two Islands romances, Andrew remarked that he had come pretty close to being a Wilcox himself. Abel, not knowing the meaning of the word *modesty,* retorted, "Sure a better man if you'd been one!"

Abel always spoke his mind. About fifty Indians, mostly from Pleasant Point, in the United States, visited Inner Wood Island every summer, making baskets or killing gulls for their feathers. Abel did not like the latter practice. One day he caught the American visitors at it, so he gave one of them a healthy kick in the behind.

"Be careful," said the Indian, "there's a crowd of us here."

Undaunted by the threat, Abel replied sharply, "I'm a crowd myself!"

Abel carried a cane. But he did not approve of the way one boy carried his. He took a surprise swipe at the lad. The boy quickly told Abel he would tell his father on him.

"Deuce, Devil," cried the sturdy Wilcox, "I'll lick you and your father, too!"

Abel had long hair, having it cut only once a year. His flowing locks could well have resulted in this remark an islander once made about such men. "My gosh, they're always combin' it.

Combin' all the time. I dunno how they can stand it. Why, I only comb my hair once a year, and it damn near kills me!"

One cold and snowy March night Abel and his good wife, Melie, went to bed early and were soon asleep. Abel had a vivid dream. In it he saw a ship aground in a cove close by, its sails flapping wildly in the wind. He woke up with a start and told his wife. "Just a dream, Abel," Melie said. "Go back to sleep." He tried, but as soon as he fell asleep, he had the very same dream. Three times this happened. This was too much for Abel. He climbed out of bed and started to dress. Melie woke up. "Abel," she said, "you must be crazy. It's a terribly wild night. Come back to bed."

Abel refused and headed out into the storm. He made his way down the trail to the cove. Through the driving snow, he saw the wreck below and got out his boat in haste. Now, the captain of the ship was a Christian man. He had prayed three times that someone would come to help him and his crew. A seaman stood beside him on the slanting deck, holding up a flickering lantern. Then they saw Abel's boat coming to the rescue. "Thank God!" cried the captain as he and his crew grabbed the pitching craft.

In all, six men climbed into Abel's boat. He took them to his house and showed them into the warm parlour. When she saw what had happened, poor Melie almost had hysterics. But all was well, and Abel's nightmare had a happy ending.

That was not the only time Abel Wilcox had such a vision. Some years later he was over at Seal Cove, felling trees and cutting wood at his logging camp. He woke up one morning and told his loggers, "I've been to the back of Grand Manan. There's been a wreck there, back of Big Head."

"But you've not been out of your bunk, Abel," cried one of his men.

"I was out of my body, boys," he replied. "I saw the ship, but I didn't go out to it. I was so tired I needed you all to come and help." His men believed him. They raced to Big Head, and, sure enough, there was a ship aground, a vessel from Lubec.

In 1917, at age ninety, Abel Wilcox died of the measles. In his will he left his land divided among his family. When his house was abandoned later, it was used from time to time by itinerant fishermen.

～

Orville and Eugene Wilcox were Abel's sons. Eugene lived on Inner Wood Island, fished off Outer Wood. Early in 1939 a traveller came by, selling sewing machines. Being hospitable souls, the

Wilcoxes invited him to stay for dinner. Mrs. Wilcox said they just had fish for dinner. But to Eugene she whispered, "If he's a good man, it's good enough for him. If he's a bad man, it's too good for him!"

Flounder has never been popular on any of the islands. Eugene and his family were having flounder for dinner one night when company dropped in unexpectedly. The children were quickly warned not to say the word *flounder,* and eventually everyone sat down. In the middle of the meal Eugene's son Lee wanted a second helping. He thought quickly and piped up, "Would you please pass the ... the ... scorpion?" Of course, he had no idea what a scorpion was. Everyone laughed, and the rest of the family got into the habit of asking for scorpion whenever they were out visiting and were served any fish. The joke was reversed one day when Lee was passed a plate with a small scorpion on it. It turned him so that he never made the remark again.

Eugene was known as a man of few words. His nephew Theal Wilcox wanted to borrow his uncle's gun, so he telephoned Eugene. The conversation was short and to the point.

"'Lo," said Eugene.

"This you, Uncle Gene?"

"Yep."

"Kin I borrow your musket shooter?"

"Nope."

Eugene never spoke a single word more than necessary. When one of his neighbours asked how many herring he had caught, his reply was blunt. "Don't know. Didn't count 'em."

Another man was a lot more talkative than Eugene. When his young bull disappeared, he raced over to his neighbours and cried, "Did you see mah two-year-old bull? Half white, all black, a six-thread rope around mah neck. That's me, ah belong to heem!"

~

Anyone who knew the folks on Two Islands will never forget them. Ben Lorimer and Ernest Joy of Inner Wood; Ernest's neighbour Reuben Wilcox; Theodore, Harl, and Frank Griffin (Frank's house on Big Hill burned down); Delia Griffin, who was christened Cordelia after King Lear's good daughter; Irwin Ramsdell, who moved into the old Reuben Wilcox place and married Roscoe Wilcox's daughter Rena; Sherman and Annie Griffin, who actually lived in Frank Griffin's home until it burned down; Mariner Wilcox; Lee and Carrie Wilcox, who moved into Mariner's place; Mariner's son Byron; Bartel Anderson, who eventually bought Mariner's house and really fixed it up. (He later drowned, and his widow and their sons, Gerald and Nelson, moved to Seal Cove. She remarried, to Don Wilcox, and lived on Grand Manan until her death.)

The old families never lost their connections with Two Islands. The Wilcoxes owned most of the western end of Inner Wood Island; the Greens owned most of the eastern end.

In the 1930s Lee Wilcox, who had been served the scorpion, sold his home to a writer from California who used it as a summer place. The writer visited Spain in winter, researching a book on the history of Spanish colonization in the Americas. I never knew if the book was finished, but I do know the county took over the property for unpaid taxes.

Billy Guptill was a young man when he moved from Grand Manan to Inner Wood Island and started putting up herring. He built a house and married Lee and Archer Wilcox's sister, Kathleen. Kathleen was a determined woman. She was known as Aunt Kitty.

One day the schoolmarm, Belva Daggett, was passing by the Guptill house, carrying her box camera. She noticed Aunt Kitty out in the yard and asked if she could take her picture. This antagonized Aunt Kitty to no end, and she replied, "No, no. You'll be some smart if you get mah picture!" She quickly ducked out of sight.

Now, if Kathleen Guptill was determined, she had finally run into someone else equally so. Belva made up her mind then and there to accept the challenge and get Aunt Kitty's picture. Belva had a good look at the lay of the land. Behind the house was a large lilac bush. She knew that Aunt Kitty was in the habit of carrying pigswill from her Uncle Eugene's place to her own. Belva thought that if she could hide behind the lilacs, she would catch Aunt Kitty unaware and get the picture. Sure enough, down the path came Kathleen Guptill with two buckets of swill in her hands. Belva aimed her camera and took the picture.

Aunt Kitty was mad, make no mistake about it. Someone had outsmarted her, and, what's worse, it was the schoolteacher. Without a moment's hesitation she hurled a bucket of swill at Belva. The schoolteacher was a mess when she arrived home at Eugene Wilcox's place, where she boarded. Her hair was in filthy tangles, and she smelled to high heaven. But she had her picture, made all the more precious by the effort.

A week or so later Belva received the prints back from the developers, and the picture of Aunt Kitty was a winner. Anxious to show it off, Belva rapped on the window of Aunt Kitty's kitchen. But still angry, Aunt Kitty turned away.

Later I asked to see the famous photo. But it was not to be. Somehow Kitty had gone over to her brother's house, snuck into Belva's room, and taken the offending snap. It was never seen again.

Belva was only one of many teachers who had wonderful adventures on Two Islands. Mary Shepherd Clift, Eunice Daggett, no relation to Belva, and Ena Bleumortier all taught there at one time or another. They were all natives of Grand Manan, and though they all boarded on Two Islands, Hugh Shepherd, a fisherman, rowed them across to Seal Cove on Friday afternoons to take them home for the weekends. The school population on Two Islands was about forty-five.

～

The men mainly fished between the two islands, at the northeastern shore or at the southern end. At first they used only dories, but as time went by, they used boats with outboard motors. When the herring catch started to fall off, a few folks moved to Grand Manan. To venture out farther, the fishermen needed larger boats. But there were no harbours or even breakwaters around Two Islands to accommodate such boats. Seal Cove had a proper harbour, and when a new wharf was built there, the fate of Two Islands was sealed. The population dropped slowly.

Other factors hastened the decline. There were no medical services, so sick people went to Seal Cove, most of them staying at Grace Ingersoll's house, where many a baby was born. There was also a doctor on Grand Manan.

And more stores. For a while the store back of Abel's old house hung on. At one time Cassie, Abel's grandson, actually sold groceries at prices lower than the stores on Grand Manan, but he, too, saw the writing on the wall and moved to Seal Cove, where Gerald Anderson had a business.

At the beginning of the migration, in the late twenties, a lot of Two Islanders settled around Seal Cove Creek, some finding work at the machine shop. The old shop was owned in turn by George Russell, Howard Zwicker, Wallace Green, and Samuel Guptill.

Others left as well, such as Chester and Viola Green. They had lived on Inner Wood Island and then Outer Wood. When their house burned down, they did not bother to rebuild or relocate on Two Islands. Instead they took the path of least resistance and joined the trek to Grand Manan. Eventually no one even cared to board the schoolteacher. The enrolment dropped to five students, and the school was finally closed; Harry Chapman was the last teacher.

Ben Lorimer (left) and Theal Wilcox were the last two residents to leave Two Islands. Ben moved to Seal Cove but travelled back and forth to Inner Wood Island to take care of Theal, who was dying. Theal refused to leave.

A local resident named Merlin Green claimed he saw a face at his window one night. He described it as the face of the devil, horns and all. Perhaps the name of that devil was Progress, the erosion of a way of life.

Archer Coy Wilcox, another one of Abel's grandsons, had served in the forces during World War II. He turned his summer home at Red Point into a year-round house. From there he could look across the water to the isle of his birth, the isle where he had spent so many happy years. So much of his poetry must have been inspired by that view and by his memories of Two Islands.

～

How many people from Seal Cove have made their way slowly to that little church and paused to gaze at the school and the empty houses and see them as they once were, full of life and love and laughter. Two Islanders still own their land—no money could buy it from them. Once a year they gather together and hold a service of reunion in the old deserted church with its proud concrete steps and its old, rusty electric generator. What do they think of their islands now?

"Come on, Ina, let's have lunch!" With a start, I found myself in the old abandoned cemetery just across from the church. I opened the gate of the well-kept fence and walked towards my friends. But my thoughts were elsewhere. I was thinking of Theal Wilcox. He was the last person to come off Two Islands, in 1957. Dear old Theal. They had to use force to make him leave his home.

Ghostly Goings-on

She was a tall and kindly soul
No graces did she lack
She wore a shawl from head to toe
The Woman Dressed in Black

"Ina," said Victor Parker, "you'll remember my dad, Bob? He was telegraph operator and chief electrician on Grand Manan in the early twenties and the thirties." I nodded. "Well, Dad sent me out, together with several other men, to help lay the cable to White Head by way of Ross Island and Cheney Island.

"It was a beautiful summer day, and the boys were busy digging holes in a straight line across Cheney, to put the posts in. All of a sudden we noticed a man walkin' towards us. You couldn't help noticing him, for he was dressed much different than the men's attire of those days. He had on a bowler hat, a shirt with a celluloid collar, a long tie, striped pants, a swallow-tailed coat, grey spats, and patent-leather shoes. Quite a dandy. He wore only one black glove, on his right hand."

As Victor was repairing my television, he was telling me the story of old man Cheney, one of the many ghost tales of Grand Manan and its archipelago. Most people are superstitious to a degree, but on an island, any island, they are more so. I can remember Highland tales that kept me awake nights when I was a young lass in Scotland, the stories of the ghosts of the Outer Hebrides. These superstitions are rooted in the ancient folk tales passed from one generation to another.

First, there are the superstitions that govern everyday life on Grand Manan. If you enter a deserted house and find a rocking chair, do not rock it, for that will bring you bad luck. When you push a boat out from shore, always turn to the right. If you turn to the left, bad luck will follow in your wake. If you are busy at household chores and happen to drop a dishcloth, that means a caller. If it falls and spreads out, the caller will be a woman; if it lands in a heap, the caller will be a man. A broom falling across a doorway signifies a visitor as well. Keep an eye on the cutlery, too. If you drop two knives, you will have a fight; if you drop two forks, you will go to a wedding.

Fishermen, especially, are a superstitious lot. Old fishermen never started to build weirs on Friday. When one man defied the taboo, beginning construction of a weir on that day and completing it exactly a week later, the old idea was reinforced. You see, that weir was never seined. Friday marks the day of the Crucifixion, and perhaps that fact lay at the root of this belief.

Fishermen are suspicious of corduroy coats, too. In the fifties Robert's nephew Burton Small got his crew together to seine herring at sea. One of the men wore a corduroy coat. "Leave that at home, man," cried Burton. But the lad refused. When the boat arrived at Canso, there was nothing but trouble for two nights. The seine was torn up, they lost a huge school of herring, there was engine trouble, and they parted a ring in the seine. That was the last straw. There were six men aboard the boat, but Burton knew what was causing the problems. "That coat has to go right now," he said. "If you want to save it, mail it home!"

A brand new truck arrived to pick up their small catch of herring, so the lad gave his corduroy coat to the driver for safekeeping until the boat came ashore. For the next two nights the crew was the luckiest at sea, seining a phenomenal catch. The boat was loaded to the gunwales when it docked at the wharf. The driver of the truck, meanwhile, had met with a nasty accident. All of Burton's crew vowed, "There, by darn, there'll be no more corduroy coats aboard this boat!" There never were, and it was a lucky boat for the rest of its days.

～

Sawyer's Lumber Camp, on the way to Dark Harbour, was a going concern in the 1930s. After logging, the men relaxed over a hot drink and a game of cards. Four of them were intent on their game in the lumber shack, with the door securely hooked. All of a sudden the hook lifted, and the door swung open slowly. A huge hound, more than four feet tall, padded into the shack, looked at each of the men, then turned and walked out without a sound. One of the men swore loudly, leapt to his feet, and hurled the cards into the fire. He rushed to the still-open door. In the damp earth outside, there was not a single paw mark.

The ghostly tales date back to the earliest settlers. During the time of the Fenian Raids two spies were sent to Canada, and they spent the winter at Hay Point, back of Grand Manan. Reuben Wilcox, an ancestor of Abel Wilcox's, was living at Deep Cove. There was a knock on his door, and a stranger showed him two guns he wanted to sell. Reuben said he needed only one, which he bought. The next summer Reuben was in Eastport, Maine. An old friend told him that two men had gone to Grand Manan in the fall, but only one had come back. It was thought that the stranger had killed his companion.

In the fifties Burton Small's boat had a run of bad luck because one crew member was wearing a corduroy coat.

Years passed, and one early-winter day Orlando Joy and Wellen Wilcox were both in camp at Hay Point. Already there was a foot of snow on the ground, with a hard crust. One of the boys was lying on the cot; the other sat at the table. They were chatting about the Fenians and whether or not their ghosts inhabited these parts. All of a sudden both of them heard the crunch of heavy footsteps just outside the door. "Here they come, Welly!" cried Orlando. They heard the grunts and heavy breathing of a man, as if he bore a heavy burden. The footsteps moved away to the bluff. There was a loud cry of someone falling down and down. Both men packed and left. Neither ever stayed there again.

Of course, there are stories that may have been only coincidence, but they still leave an impression. Two women from Seal Cove were in Boston. For a lark they visited a fortune-teller. The message they were told was chilling, but they both laughed it off. According to the mystic, the man who delivered eggs to their home was going to cut his throat. When they returned home, it had happened—the man was dead.

Archer Wilcox, the poet, told me a story that took place in the thirties, when his family lived in Meredith Wilson's home on Inner Wood Island. There was a knock at the door, and his sister-in-law, Carrie, thought it was the children. "Go away," she yelled. But the knock was repeated three times. By then Carrie was frightened. "Lord, give me strength to open the door," she said to herself. Finally she did.

There was an old woman on the doorstep. It was Carrie's grandmother, who lived in Rockland, Maine. As Carrie stared at her, she disappeared into thin air. Carrie was terrified.

Before she had died, the grandmother had said to her husband, "I want to see my dear Carrie." Then she had gone into her bedroom. There was a scream, and the old woman dropped her lamp and fell to the floor.

It is said that Carrie had psychic powers. When her family moved to Ernest Joy's house, she claimed she often saw visions of her mother, who had lived in that very same place.

Two Islands had a ghost. Known as The Woman in Black, she was reputed to be the spirit of Mrs. Ned Fitzgerald, who had settled on Inner Wood Island in the early nineteenth century. Her husband, so the story goes, had been a brute who beat his children for any offence. His grave is marked by a cairn of stones. Mrs. Fitzgerald, on the other hand, was a kind soul, or so it seems.

Cassie Wilcox, Archer's brother, told one early reporter that she was tall, stately, and dressed from head to toe in black, with a black shawl that graced her tiny frame. No record of tragedy was ever linked to her appearances. In fact, a child named Muriel Wilcox would have tumbled over the cliff facing Grand Manan had the cold hands of The Woman in Black not yanked her back from the precipice.

It was a different kind of ghost that Alfred Wilcox encountered. Alfred was on his way back from a neighbour's house when he looked behind him and saw the Deerstalker of Inner Wood Island. A man was following him, carrying something that looked like a deer over his shoulder. The ghost entered the house that he had just left. Shortly after, Alfred's uncle died. Fortunately no one else ever saw the ghostly hunter and his prey.

～

Just opposite Woodwards Cove lies Nantucket Island, abandoned for years, until the 1970s. People say a ghost wanders through the ruins of the old buildings and along the shore. The story originated at the turn of the century, when the island was inhabited.

A woman lived there who had a pleasant disposition but homely looks. A successful writer of magazine and newspaper articles, she had never married, even though she had a romantic soul. In such an isolated spot, she had few opportunities to meet men. This, however, did not deter her. One day she answered a "lonelyhearts" advertisement. She developed a flourishing correspondence with the man on the other side of the ad, and the two decided to meet and get married.

They met for the first time at the railway station in Saint John. Well, perhaps he got a surprise—she was a large masculine woman. But he was not too comely, either, with a shock of bright red hair, and was rather hard of hearing. Nonetheless, they could not deny their true love for each other and were soon married. They settled on Nantucket Island, where they farmed sheep, cows, and hens.

Soon they were blessed with children. It seemed that their life together would be long and happy. Then tragedy struck. Two men were clamming on the island when they heard a shot break the stillness of the quiet afternoon. Then they saw the poor woman running down the shore, where she found the body of her husband. For some reason he had shot himself. Soon after, she moved away and lived alone until her death. Her spirit still walks that island.

～

Now, Grand Mananers are particular about their ghosts. They do not put up with any phoney manifestations. The Temple Knoll woods was supposedly home to a ghost, as well as many practical jokes. Temple Knoll is situated between two cemeteries on the road from Woodwards Cove to Castalia.

The mysterious deer of Temple Knoll was hardly a ghost. Gordon (Ben) Polkinhorn was a real wag. He made a life-size deer out of wood, painted it, and set it up in a clearing in the woods. At dusk a neighbour was driving by and noticed the stately animal. He got his son, and armed with guns, they raced back to the clearing. "Shoot, boy!" cried the father. The boy fired, but nothing moved. "Come on, son, shoot again. Quick, get it before it moves!" The boy fired again, and the "deer" tumbled in the darkness. Needless to say, the catch was good only for kindling in the kitchen stove.

Two fake spirits laid the ghost of Temple Knoll to rest once and for all. Two boys were keeping a close eye on another lad who often visited his girlfriend in Castalia. About midnight he usually walked home to Woodwards Cove.

Now, the other two boys knew this lad was a bit on the nervous side, so they decided to play a trick one night. They grabbed two sheets, headed to Temple Knoll, and hid behind some bushes. About the witching hour along came their quarry, bravely whistling a happy tune to give himself courage until he was safely by the dreaded graveyards. When he came to the cemeteries, the two "ghosts" rose from the graves and howled loudly. The pedestrian took to his heels across fields and woods and soon disappeared from sight.

There were a good number of stories about ghosts in the graveyards, mostly made up, but there was one that had been repeated several times. At Temple Knoll a light often appeared mysteriously in one of the cemeteries. The frightened youth's tale of his hair-raising experience led to an investigation, and it was soon discovered that the mysterious light was actually a reflection from the Fish Fluke Point Light shining through the bushes onto a polished headstone.

Victor paused, switched on the television, and a perfect picture lit up the screen. "There, that's got it!"

"What happened then?" I asked.

"Well," said Victor, taking a seat, "this fella walked right up to me bold as brass and asked who was in charge. 'Me,' I said. He held out his right hand, the one with the glove, and we shook hands. That hand sure felt funny. It was as hard as stone. He asked me what we were doing, so I told him, but he didn't seem to understand. 'Tellerpone lines?' he asked. 'What on earth is a tellerpone?' He took off his bowler hat and scratched his head, then, putting it back on, stated, 'You have no right here. Who gave you permission to dig these holes?'

"I explained that the government owned the right-of-way and that Glen McLaughlin, who owned the island, had given us permission. 'McLaughlin? I know of no such man,' the man said. 'I own this island, and I forbid you, any of you, to dig any more holes! Good day.' He doffed his bowler hat briefly and strode way from us up to the old deserted house.

"Well, Ina, I was dumbfounded. I realized I should have got his name, so a few of us went up to the old house. There was no one there. There was no sign of him anywhere on the island. Ours was the only boat, so how in the devil had he reached Cheney Island?

"That night I reported to Father what had happened, over the phone. 'You get over here right away, Victor!' he yelled, and hung up. When I got home, Dad made me tell everything over again. He paused, shook his head several times, and then said quietly, 'Victor, that was old man Cheney you talked with. He's been dead for over a hundred years!'

"I can tell you that fair shook me. A fella named Cronk said he also saw old Cheney, only that was on Ross Island. He followed him, as his tracks could be seen on the beach, but then they faded away, and Cronk lost sight of him."

Victor stood, gathered his tools, and made for the door.

"But are you sure it was old man Cheney?" I asked.

"Oh yes, one thing I forgot to mention, Ina. Remember I told you I shook hands with him ... and how there was a black leather glove on his right hand ... and how strange it felt?"

"Yes, I do."

Victor paused in the doorway. "Dad told me one more thing about old man Cheney. He'd had an accident, a serious one at that. His right hand was artificial, made of wood!"

Change

I must leave these memories
And let them go at last,
For I can never go again
Back to the happy past.
—Mary Pushee

Alas, memory is fleeting. So it's not surprising that much of Grand Manan's unique heritage has been lost over the centuries. Luckily islanders realized how much of their history was slipping away before it was too late. In the early 1960s Elmer Wilcox, Keith Ingersoll, the principal of the high school, and many others started working towards the establishment of a museum. The Grand Manan Museum, a Centennial project, opened at Grand Harbour in 1967. Its displays include Allan Moses's collection of mounted birds, a marine gallery with a lighthouse, and a geological exhibit.

In 1931 Buchanan Charles, a summer visitor, had formed the first Grand Manan historical society. Islanders reorganized it in 1963, and it is active today, publishing the *Grand Manan Historian*. Some books have also recorded island history—Keith Ingersoll's anthology *On This Rock* and museum curator Eric Allaby's *Grand Manan*.

Despite these efforts, a good deal of island history has passed into oblivion. Many Grand Mananers sold their possessions to hungry tourists for a song. Irene Titus, the wife of high-school custodian Charles Titus, had several pieces of valuable antique furniture, including a bed spring made of ropes and an entire mahogany bedroom set assembled with wooden pegs. Aunt Jennie Lambert of North Head had a Royal ironstone milk pitcher that came from the *Lord Ashburton.*

In 1973 the Ganderton house burned to the ground. This home had been standing since the early 1820s, containing so much that should have found its way into the museum. It was known as the Ganong place, because the chocolate family had used it as a summer retreat for many years. I remember the Polkinhorn house, also built in the 1820s—its two huge fireplaces, its hand-hewn beams, and its wide floor boards. A few families had a real history. Ingalls Head, for example, took its name from the Ingalls family, whose early life was dramatized on the television series *Little House on the Prairies.*

Some real treasures have been found along the shores and in the old houses. Douglas Harris, a stranger from away, was

The Cook house at Grand Harbour is an example of some of the period architecture on the island. A few other fine homes have burned to the ground, their history lost forever.

building a sea wall in 1972 and came across a two-hundred-year-old penny. Other precious coins have been found on Grand Manan—Money Cove was named for those old pieces.

In the mid-sixties Ronald Brown of Seal Cove discovered two ancient medicine bottles while fixing the chimney of the McLaughlin home, also in Seal Cove. One bottle's label read, "Hall's Vegetable Sicilian Hair Renewer—1866. Reuben P. Hall, M.D. Price: $1.00." The second bottle had the following: "Professor Small's AMBROSIAL NECTAR. Tonic for weak stomachs, bilious complaints, etc.... This medicine is physical! Prepared by E. G. Small, Wilson's Beach, Campobello, N.B. Price: $1.00." I was especially interested in that second bottle, as a souvenir rather than for its curative powers. You see, the Smalls of Campobello are distantly related to the Smalls of Grand Manan.

Over the years I watched the face of the island change. At North Head, for instance, Joseph Gaskill's store, where the Red Cross group had met in the 1940s, was made into apartments; the Lahey store, a millinery store. The Ross Russell General Store changed hands, and the shoemaker's establishment was closed down. There is a modern customs house and a modern post office. In

Grand Harbour, there is a new Bank of Nova Scotia—the building of the first bank on the island, the Bank of New Brunswick, burned down. And in Castalia, there is a well-stocked liquor store.

~

Before the outlet was opened in 1967, a lot of boats and travellers brought liquor to the island from Nova Scotia and the United States. Alcohol had always been available: at one time, the Steamboat Wharf agent at North Head sold liquor for a commission of twenty-five cents a bottle. Slowly, however, the New Brunswick government became wise to the tax dollars leaving the province.

Time and again islanders have demonstrated their resourcefulness and their independence from the provincial powers-that-be. Some remnants of those qualities are long gone. During Prohibition, there were rumrunners aplenty. After one ran aground, a number of the smart young set hid bottles of liquor in a tombstone in the graveyard across from St. Paul's Anglican Church in Grand Harbour. The headstone was pyramidal in design and had a movable metal plate that hid a hollow core. Any thirsty passer-by could pause in the cemetery, slide up the tablet, bring forth a bottle, and have a hearty swig of spirit present. This graveyard became quite dilapidated, and a group under the direction of Harold Small, Anita and P.M.'s son, worked hard to restore it.

Not everyone was happy when the province opened the liquor store. One man was in the local barbershop getting a haircut and a shave. He was chatting with the barber when the welfare officer entered. Then the conversation switched to the abuses of welfare as the barber took out his straight razor. "Look at those two lads," said the customer in the chair, lifting his head so the barber could shave his neck. "Both of them are on welfare, both on the way to the liquor store to pick up booze!" All three men looked out the window of the barbershop as the two boys disappeared into the liquor outlet.

Later that afternoon the welfare officer met the loquacious customer on the street. "You sure like to live dangerously," he remarked.

"What do you mean?" asked the man, rubbing his clean-shaven face with some satisfaction. He hadn't even been nicked once.

"Why, those two boys you were talking about while you were getting a shave, didn't you know they're the barber's sons!"

~

Some things have never changed on Grand Manan. Men and boys continue to be swallowed by the sea. I was personally concerned when Beverly Boynton was rescued in 1971 because he had come to school to me. Beverly and his partner, Arthur Middleton, were in their thirty-five-foot boat when a freak swell tipped the vessel and threw Arthur into the water. Arthur, the father of seven children, drowned, and his body was never found. Beverly swam clear, but he could not hold on to his boat, which was fortunate, for it was swept ashore and dashed to pieces against the rocks.

While swimming away, Beverly caught his arm in the line of a lobster trap, which held him fast. Clifton Taylor and his nephew Lawrence were fishing nearby and came to Beverly's rescue but were unable to get him free of the line. In fact, their boat nearly foundered as well. Clifton radioed for a second boat, and his brother Wesley and a friend, Francis Stanley, arrived to lend a hand. Eventually they winched Beverly out of the sea, half drowned, with a cracked jaw. He spent twelve days in hospital recovering from the ordeal. Beverly Boynton has never fished again.

A Sailor Who Came Home from the Sea

Home is the fisherman ... home is the rover
Home is the sailor ... his voyage over
May he rest quietly, may he rest peacefully
May he rest in peace near the restless sea

Robert was feeling ill. He asked me for a cup of coffee but took only small sips. It was late September 1976, and my lifelong friend Connie was visiting from Moncton. She helped make breakfast, but Robert ate nothing. Dr. Dapena came but was unable to relieve Robert of his pain, so Connie and I rushed him to the late-morning boat. An ambulance met us at Blacks Harbour and sped us to Saint John.

All the while, I thought of the wonderful moments of our life together ... of that frosty January in 1927, when Robert held me gently but firmly, guiding me stealthily over the ice ... of our berrying expeditions and how Robert paid so much so I could have my favourite berries ... of our adventures in the old Ford.

My mind filled with less pleasant memories, too ... the day in 1944 that Maureen and I boarded the ferry for a long, lonely stay in Saint John. How foolish I'd been. After my return our marriage was as happy as ever, with Robert and I spending winters in Florida, summers on glorious Grand Manan.

Suddenly I was filled with pride. Robert was one of the most successful men on Grand Manan. By the 1950s he owned two herring factories, both going concerns. But never had I been as proud of him as I had on Maureen's wedding day. Maureen had met a young graphic designer, and theirs was a whirlwind courtship. On June 28, 1952, they were married in the Anglican church in Saint John. Maureen looked radiant, and Robert was as handsome as ever. They smiled into each other's eyes as they came up the aisle. Robert walked like a king.

But now I knew that Robert and I were entering the last phase of our life together. I was sixty-nine, and he was nearing eighty-one. In Saint John he was diagnosed as having cancer of the prostate. Because of his heavy smoking, he had also developed emphysema. This, together with his age, made an operation impossible. I was devastated, but I knew I had to get him home.

The ferry was due for a winter refit, and the last trip was scheduled for Saturday morning. It took forever to engage an ambulance to Blacks Harbour. When we did, we realized that we would never catch the ferry. After a series of frantic phone calls, authorities delayed the sailing. I was never so glad to see North Head—the trip had seemed an eternity.

Maureen, I, and Robert decided that it would be best for him to go to Ocean View Lodge. Until that moment Robert had not realized he was terminally ill. I had to tell him he had cancer. Being the same brave fisherman I had met fifty years ago, he just squeezed my hand and said nothing.

～

I cannot speak too highly of Ocean View Lodge. When the new hospital was built in 1971, the board of directors realized Grand Manan would also need an institution for chronically ill and elderly patients. As usual, the funding presented the greatest hurdle. As usual, the problem was solved. The lodge came about thanks to both government and private support. The provincial government gave the board a generous grant, and Faye Russo of Boston, formerly a Gaskill, and her husband donated the land. I'll always remember the Russos. The day Sam Greenlaw was confirmed, they drove him to the Anglican Church of the Ascension in their large black car. For years Sam said, "The Lord sent for Elijah to take him to heaven in a flaming chariot, but He sent for me in a Cadillac!"

Quite a few islanders donated money to the construction of Ocean View Lodge because up to now many old people had to go to nursing homes in Pennfield, near Blacks Harbour, or to homes up the Saint John River Valley in Norton or Hampton, wherever there was a vacancy. This made family visits awkward.

Ocean View Lodge opened in September 1974. It is a modern building with all the latest equipment. It faces Swallowtail Light and also has a lovely view of Castalia shore. There are maple trees and flowers and ornamental bushes and bird feeders on the spacious grounds.

It has a dining room with a spectacular view, recreation areas where patients can watch TV, play piano, enjoy a game of checkers. There is a Sunday church service, as well as plenty of socials organized by churches and community groups. And everybody's birthday is celebrated. Most important of all, it is staffed by excellent island nurses and nurse's aids who give high-quality care.

Robert was in Ocean View for eight months, taking nothing but a little water for three. Maureen came to see him at Christmas and at Easter, the last time she ever saw him alive. The doctors had told me Robert would live only three months, but they failed to take into account his fighting spirit.

During my visits to the lodge, I had a chance to gather many stories and to eavesdrop on some unusual conversations. Canon H. Sherman Shepherd of the Anglican church was born on Inner Wood Island. After his wife died, he returned to Grand Manan and spent his last days at the lodge. His niece Elaine was working at Ocean View, and she always called him Uncle Sherman or Uncle Sherm.

One dear old lady from St. Stephen was a patient at Ocean View. She was a friendly soul. One morning she met Canon Sherman in the hall and called out, "Good morning, Uncle Sherm!" The Canon grunted and walked right by. The woman thought that the Canon was either not sociable or hard of hearing. She decided it was the latter. So she repeated the greeting on several occasions, with the same result.

One day, however, the old clergyman stopped, looked the old woman in the eye, and said, "Lady, I am *not* your Uncle Sherm any more than you are Queen Elizabeth's aunt."

One time Canon Shepherd said to me, "There are a great many good and religious people on this island, Ina, but not much Christianity." I wondered what good ol' Uncle Willie would have retorted.

Through the winter I travelled the eight-mile trip to see Robert every day, until early spring. I was raking leaves and suddenly passed out. I didn't know until later that I had had a heart attack. The staff at Ocean View told Robert that I had a cold.

In mid-May I went to see him. That afternoon will never leave my mind. My neighbour Mona Small was with me. Robert was a pale shadow of his former self—he weighed less than fifty pounds.

"Time to go, Ina," Mona whispered. Robert's eyes were closed, and his breathing was shallow. "Murray Clift is driving Harold up to the Head, so he can take us. You leave your car. I'll spend the night with you." This made me wonder—Mona was a nurse. It seemed to be so much trouble for Murray and Harold.

~

The phone rang about midnight. We'd just gone to bed, and Mona jumped up and answered it. "Who's that?" I asked.

"Just Ocean View, Ina. They've given Robert a needle, and he's resting quietly." I settled into a fitful sleep.

The phone rang again. It was three in the morning, May 12, 1977. Mona answered; she listened and said nothing. She hung up and came over and sat on my bed. There were tears in her eyes. I knew.

"It's all over, Ina." Dear Mona. How could she know that it would never be over.

I received a ground swell of sympathy and support. Dear Connie, who had lost her Russell two years before, rushed to the island. She and her sister, Ruth, had packed, raced to Blacks Harbour, and barely managed to catch the early-morning ferry. On the same trip were our daughter, Maureen, her husband, and their two beautiful daughters, Angela and Roxanne. Walter's daughters, Mary and Jetta—Walter, too, was dead—my sister-in-law Izetta McAllan, and my niece and nephew Catherine and William came soon after.

Robert's funeral service was held at St. Paul's Anglican Church, and the church was full. He was laid to rest at the Anglican Church of the Ascension Cemetery. As one of the ministers read Tennyson's "Crossing the Bar," my eyes filled with tears. I looked up and saw a flock of gulls swoop low over the graveside. Perhaps they, too, were paying their last respects to a brave sailor and fisherman.

Epilogue

It is my beloved homeland ...
It is where I want to lie ...

September 13, 1977. I closed and locked the door on our empty house. My heart was just as empty. I was alone. I would take both happy and sad memories with me, but nothing would ever be the same again.

The next morning was bright and sunny. I stood on the deck of the *Grand Manan* and took one last look at the island. My heart was sore. I knew every nook, every house, nearly every person. I had said goodbye to some dear old friends.

Here I had met my Robert ... so long ago ... and here he had left me ... after so many years of struggle and accomplishment. How resolute he was.

How well I know my island ... the rugged cliffs and shores ... so formidable in the beginning ... so welcoming later on. The cool sweet summers when the wild flowers burst into passionate bloom ... the crisp winters that chilled your marrow until you shared the comfort of a friendly hearth ... the fog so damp and ghostlike ... until the solemn blasts of The Whistle call out to passing ships, "Danger ahead ... take care!"

Take care indeed, fishermen of Grand Manan. Never forget your proud heritage.

"Take care ... take care." Almost a benediction to those who leave the island ... the proud young graduates of the high school ... itself a lighthouse to a better future.

"Take care ... take care." Like a tide, it calls them back ... to the island they will always love ... to Seal Cove and Southern Head ... to North Head and Swallowtail ... to Whale Cove and to the Southern Cross ... to the shores of Grand Manan. My island.

A loud blast of the ship's whistle brought me out of my reverie with a start. The lines were cast off, and the ferry pulled slowly away from its slip. I gazed as long as I could at the shrinking steeple of the Anglican Church of the Ascension and the cemetery back of it. Tears filled my eyes. It would be my resting place also, beside Robert.

Soon I will come home, at peace, my wanderings over.

Only then will I no longer be a stranger from away.